I0742446

INTENDED BONDMATES

BOOKS BY D. LIEBER

Minte and Magic
The Exiled Otherkin
The Assassin's Legacy

Intended Fates
Intended Bondmates
Intended Strangers
Intended Enemies

Council of Covens
Dancing with Shades
In Search of a Witch's Soul

Also by D. Lieber
Conjuring Zephyr
Once in a Black Moon
A Very Witchy Yuletide
The Treason of Robyn Hood
The Curse of Moonseed Manor
The Goblin King's Mischief
The Winter Sorcerer and the Summer Witch
Bitten by the North Wind
The Glass Moth

INTENDED BONDMATES

BOOK ONE OF INTENDED FATES

D. LIEBER

Ink & Magick, LLC
Kenosha, Wisconsin
contact@inkandmagick.com

Hardcover ISBN: 978-1-951239-06-0
Paperback ISBN: 978-1-7328323-7-4
Ebook ISBN: 978-1-7328323-8-1

Cover art by Black Rose Writing
Edited by Cover to Cover Editing

DEDICATION

To my parents:
Thank you for always encouraging me to try my best and
never give up.

A special thanks to my beta readers: John, Amy, Laura,
and Aunt Debbie.

1

"Wake up!" Mikhail demanded at the foot of my bed as he kicked me awake.

I cracked my sleep-crusted lids and peeked at him. He was pristine as always. His golden hair was artfully arranged, and he wore black trousers with a black waistcoat over a white shirt. His tie was the same color as his fiery-blue eyes, which squinted at me.

I didn't need the bond to tell he was irritated I wasn't already on my feet. I turned my head to look out the dingy curtains.

"It's still dark." I yawned and rolled out of bed.

He turned his back to my half-clothed state.

"Of course, it is still dark. Father and Mother would never allow us to leave if they knew where we are going," he chided like it was obvious.

"And where is that?" I asked, rubbing my eyes as I scouted my bedroom floor for a decently clean pair of pants.

He grumbled under his breath about having a

useless bondmate and then sighed. "We are going to the Wolf Council. I wrote to them a while ago to request we be unbound early, and they have granted us an audience."

The shoe I was about to pull on thumped to the floor as it slipped through my fingers. Mikhail looked over his shoulder at the sound.

"Mikhail, I know we aren't well-matched bondmates, but it isn't that long before your awakening. Can't you hold out until then?" I pleaded.

"I have been forced to suffer your presence far longer than I have patience for. I am lucky I could even find a worthy mate like Colleen with your low-class stench surrounding me like a cloud of noxious gas. You *will* accompany me to the Wolf Council and agree to be unbound from me as soon as they will allow."

As his words slashed into me, I barely felt the pain. I'd long become familiar with their sting over the last thirteen years. I stifled a sigh, resigning myself to his will as I finished dressing.

"And pack a bag. I doubt you will be returning," he ordered.

I filled my rucksack with my small supply of clothes and shouldered it. It was packed so tight I couldn't fit anything else. I even had to leave behind my hairbrush and toothbrush.

We exited the dark, quiet mansion via the servants' entrance and walked softly through the complex to the depot. The conductor waited for us inside the large, wooden structure.

"Thank you for meeting us so early. Can I rely on your discretion?" Mikhail asked the conductor.

"Of course, Sir," he assured. He motioned us

into the transportation circle and asked, "Where to?"

"Lupine City Hall," Mikhail told him.

He nodded and began whispering the spell. As the soft command flowed from his lips, the circle started to glow with yellow light. There was a blinding flash, and we stood in another circle in another depot.

As we exited the depot amongst a crowd of morning commuters, it was obvious we were no longer on his family's estate. The solid, stone structures of Lupine City were a far cry from the picturesque architecture of his family complex. Dawn was just lighting the eastern horizon as we approached the imposing edifice that was Lupine City Hall.

Our footsteps echoed off the marble floors and walls of the entrance hall. Many archways led to other rooms, and there was a marble staircase to the right.

"How may I help you?" a receptionist asked from behind a desk to the left of the entrance.

"We have an audience with the Wolf Council this morning," Mikhail explained.

"Runa and Mikhail?" the receptionist asked after consulting a schedule book.

I felt my jaw tighten as Mikhail's irritation shot through the bond. He nodded at the receptionist.

He can't stand that they put my name first.

The receptionist gave us directions to the council chambers and told us to wait until we were called. We climbed the marble staircase and took a seat outside a set of huge, polished wooden doors. I slouched beside Mikhail on the stone bench. He squinted his displeasure at my posture although he kept his criticism to himself for once. *As if I need him to rebuke me aloud to know how he's feeling.* I sighed and tried not to think too much, but my mind flew off in multiple directions.

Why is Mikhail doing this now? What's going to happen to me? I have always known he resented me for Isla's death. It's not like I really wanted to be bound with him either, but what else could I have done in that situation? I was young and impressionable, not to mention grief-stricken and scared. At least I can say I tried to be a good bondmate to him. Where can I go if they agree to unbind us? My pack won't allow me to return a failure.

A no-nonsense young man interrupted my thoughts when he opened the chamber doors and called, "Runa and Mikhail?"

My pulse quickened with Mikhail's resurfaced irritation. We stood and stepped forward.

The man met my eyes with disapproval and motioned to us. We followed him inside, and he took a seat near a long table, readying to take notes. The table was occupied by thirteen alphas in human form, one from each of the thirteen families. Two court security officers in wolf form stood guard by the door we had entered.

Three chairs faced the table. My pack's alpha sat in the chair to the left. I hadn't seen her in thirteen years, but I would recognize her presence anywhere. She turned her amber eyes on me when I reached her, and I immediately dropped to my knees and bowed my head.

She patted my head as she said my name. I glanced up, and her eyes softened with pity.

Mikhail, on the other hand, looked on in shock.

His mouth hung open at my show of respect. *I've never shown him such respectful obedience. All he ever got was resignation.*

Mikhail and I each took a seat. I resisted the urge to fidget under the oppressive stares of the alphas as I awaited my fate.

"Runa of the Mountain Meadows Clan, you were called here at the request of your bondmate, who wishes to be unbound before his awakening. Do you have anything to say?" the alpha in the middle asked.

"As always, I will bend to my faeling's will in all ways that will not compromise his safety," I responded.

The alpha nodded and turned to Mikhail.

"Mikhail of the noble house Azure, why have you requested to be unbound from Runa? Are you not to awaken in three months?"

Mikhail rose to address the council, and I ducked my head at the disrespect. Soft growls from the court security officers behind us told him to sit down. He complied smoothly and spoke as though nothing had happened.

"Honorable alphas, I submitted this request over a year ago. In my opinion, Runa and I are poorly-matched. Indeed, she was not even my intended bondmate. She was bound with me in response to tragic circumstances and as a matter of convenience. My parents should have resubmitted my application for a bondmate upon Isla's death rather than binding me with Runa."

"We understand your distress at losing your intended bondmate," an alpha toward the left chimed in. "However, that does not answer why you believe Runa is unfit. Has she not protected you as is her duty?"

"She has protected me from minor threats but has never been tested against our true enemy while bound with me. I am to be mated shortly after my awakening. I fear Runa's presence, since she is not of an equal status, may disrupt these plans."

"Mikhail, we are reluctant to grant a request that would leave you vulnerable to vampire attack so close to your awakening. Would it not be better to wait to break your bond at your awakening? Then you can realize your full magic and protect yourself. You are aware that as you approach your awakening and your magic ripens, the increased magic in your blood will make your scent stronger and more appetizing to them?" the alpha in the middle cautioned.

Mikhail waved his hand dismissively. "I am well aware. However, my parents' estate has hired wolf guards. I assure you, I am quite safe."

The alphas conferred amongst themselves for a while, and I remained painfully still. After much debate, the center alpha addressed Mikhail. "Very well, we will grant your request."

"Thank you." Mikhail bowed his head from his seat.

"Elva, do you have a proposal for what we should do with Runa?"

My alpha nodded. "It is by no fault of Runa's that she was born to a working-class pack, and even he has admitted that she has done her duty. Before she was bound with Mikhail, she was intended for another faeling of a similar class to ours. I suggest, if the faeling's family is amiable, she be bound with her intended bondmate. It is my understanding he was never bound, and his awakening is also fast approaching."

The council deliberated once more. Eventually, the center alpha said, "Excellent suggestion, Elva. We will dispatch a message to the faeling's family. In the meantime, please escort these two to be unbound."

2

The thirteen alphas of the Wolf Council dismissed us. Mikhail and I followed Elva out of the council chambers.

Mikhail's slight form bounced with every step, and satisfaction hummed through the bond.

We went downstairs and turned into the first archway on the left. The room we entered had a counter splitting it in two. On our side of the counter, benches were arranged to give visitors a place to rest while they waited. On the far side of the counter, werewolves and fae who worked in the office bustled about their duties. There were not many people in the waiting area. Two other werewolf and faeling pairs waited with their parents to be bound.

I smiled at the children. It was easy to see they were well-matched by how close they sat to each other. One pair even held hands.

I remembered being close like that with Konner. My heart leapt at the prospect of seeing him again.

Then I glanced over at Mikhail, and my hope turned sour. *I have failed as a bondmate. Why would Konner want me after all this time?*

When we were called to the counter, I stood dutifully but moved with heavy feet. Every step was a reminder that I had failed. As instructed, I faced Mikhail and took his hands. *Mikhail, what could I have done to prevent this? Why couldn't I make you trust me enough that class didn't matter? I'm sorry I'm not Isla.*

As always, the bond from me to him was cold and limp. I couldn't convey my feelings, or he ignored them if I had.

A wolf mystic and a fae priest said the words of unbinding over our joined hands. I felt the thin thread of Mikhail's emotions unbind my heart. The bond's silence left me empty. I started to shiver, my body chilled.

"Are we finished?" Mikhail asked the priest.

He nodded.

"Excellent." He turned his fiery-blue eyes on me. "I hope I never have to see you again."

My teeth started to chatter as I watched him stride from the room.

"Elva, what's happening to me?" I managed through numb lips.

The wolf mystic gave her a blanket. She wrapped it around my shoulders and sat me down on a nearby bench. "Unbinding too early can shock your body. Your drive to protect him is strong. You know he cannot yet protect himself."

She approached the counter and returned with steaming tea. "Drink this," she ordered and then left the room.

I sipped the hot liquid slowly. Warmth gradually spread through me, but the emptiness remained.

As I finished the last of the tea, Elva returned. She looked at me closely to determine my condition, then smiled. "Good news: the Fireleaf family is happy to welcome you as Konner's bondmate."

Konner still wants me? A strong desire to fill my emptiness with Konner made me throw off the blanket and shoulder my pack. I looked at Elva when she hadn't moved. "Well, when do we leave?"

She chuckled, and I followed her to the depot.

I tried to calm my excitement as Elva told the fae conductor our destination. All I could do was picture Konner's smiling face. His brown hair stuck up as cowlicks disrupted the waves. His five-year-old, brown eyes were so serious when he'd asked me to be his bondmate until his awakening. The memory of his smile at my response had haunted me. It would catch me off-guard at unpredictable times, and I'd be flooded with guilt.

The yellow light flashed, and we stood in a deserted country depot. The dirt road that led to the Fireleaf family farm was packed as though that morning's dew still held the soil together. Our boots made little sound as we hiked down the moistened path.

"You understand this is your last chance? Seeing Konner successfully through his awakening is the only way for you to rejoin the pack. I know your parents would have wanted that. Whatever mistakes were made for Mikhail to request an early unbinding, I hope you have learned from them and will do better with Konner. I want nothing more than for you to complete your rite and return to the pack. Do your best, all right, Pup?"

I bowed my head to Elva and promised to succeed.

By early afternoon, we had reached the Fireleaf farm. The medicinal herbs they grew were just starting to sprout in the spring sun. Fresh green leaves peeked above the roof of the blue farmhouse, and the trees' reaching branches formed a grove for growing plants that needed shade.

A werewolf in human form with black hair and ice-blue eyes answered our knock at the front door. His lips curled back over gleaming white teeth as he glared at me, but his menacing scowl didn't diminish his appeal. Before he could say anything, a faeling with brown hair peeked over his sturdy shoulder.

"Who is it, Rowan?" the faeling asked.

My heart jumped with excitement, then plummeted in disappointment when I realized the faeling had green eyes.

"The betrayer is here to bind with Konner," Rowan spat, making me flinch.

Elva placed a hand on my shoulder. "Remember what I said, Runa." Then she left the way we had come.

I cleared my throat and squared my shoulders. "May I speak to Master or Mistress Fireleaf, please?"

The green-eyed faeling stepped out from behind Rowan, who tensed but didn't stop him.

"I'm Wilhelm, Konner's younger brother, and you're Runa?"

A memory of a green-eyed faeling following

Konner around flashed in my mind. I nodded and tried to smile as Rowan stared daggers at me.

"This is my bondmate, Rowan. My parents are tending to seedlings. They said to make yourself at home. Konner is at the spring. Would you like me to show you the way?"

My heart jumped, alarmed that Konner wandered around unprotected.

"Wilhelm," Rowan censured. "Konner said he didn't want to be bothered."

"I thought that was just for us. She's his bond-mate. How could she be a bother?"

Rowan snorted.

"Thank you for your help. I remember the way," I said hurriedly.

I turned on my heel and walked around the house. The grove was mostly maple trees. I strode quickly and soundlessly under them, following a well-worn path to a spring.

A man lay on his stomach on a smooth rock at the spring's bank. His hand dangled over the edge, and he gently dipped his fingertips into the clear water. Mussed brown hair played around his pointed ears and splayed over half his face. His forlorn expression as he gazed into the water made my heart sink. I sucked in air to fortify myself.

His sad, brown eyes looked up at the sound and hardened. He stood quickly, yet gracefully, and stared me down.

Unlike Mikhail, Konner had grown to be healthy and strong. His broad shoulders and solid chest only momentarily distracted me from the murder in his eyes.

"Why are you here?" he demanded in a rigid voice.

The warm welcome I'd been expecting shriveled and died.

"I came to protect you until your awakening," I said helplessly.

"I've survived this long without you. What happened? Did your high-born bondmate find out you're a liar and demand an early unbinding?"

I flinched at his words and hung my head. "I thought you wanted me to come," I whispered.

"Why would I want someone who doesn't keep her promises as my bondmate? My parents accepted on my behalf. They didn't even ask me."

Hopelessness overcame me. Filling my emptiness with Konner felt like a foolish dream. *Do your best, all right, Pup?* Elva's words sounded in my mind. I made a desperate final reach for Konner. I fell to my knees and bowed my head as I would to my alpha.

"I'm sorry, Konner," I said through a lump in my throat. "I never wanted to be bound with Mikhail, but that's no excuse. I should've fought for my promise to you. I have regretted it every day for thirteen years. I'm not asking for forgiveness. But could you find it in your heart to give me a second chance? Please let me protect you until your awakening."

Silence followed my pleading, but I didn't raise my head.

"You're already here. Do what you want," he grudgingly agreed after a while.

I looked up at him gratefully, still on my knees.

He'd been staring at my bowed head and quickly averted his gaze as I met his eyes.

"I can tolerate your presence for five months. Just stay out of my way." His words were harsh, but his tone had softened a little.

"Thank you," I said sincerely.

He turned swiftly and left the grove without another word.

I followed silently, smiling to myself.

3

After shadowing Konner on the path amid the grove, we continued through the back door of the farmhouse. We passed through the kitchen and sitting room, then went upstairs to the second floor. When we reached the landing, I saw a door on the left, one straight ahead, and three on the right.

Konner pointed ahead and said, "Bathroom." Then he pointed to the center door on the right and said, "Your room."

"Which room is yours?" I asked.

He gestured to the door on the left of mine. "Wilhelm and Rowan share that one," he said as he pointed to the third door on the right. Then he went to his room and shut the door without looking back.

I sighed and shook my head at myself. *Man, I really messed up. Will this be like Mikhail all over again?* I tried not to doom my relationship with Konner to ruin by giving up, but I couldn't help feeling discouraged. *Maybe he will cool down after a while. I'll just have to prove my loyalty and commitment.*

I opened the door to my bedroom and stared, my mouth agape. The room was simple but welcoming. It was far more comfortable than my small, dirty room in the servants' wing of the Azure estate. My new room had a large bed, an armoire, and a desk with a chair. The window was big and framed in clean, pink curtains. There were doors leading to both Konner's and Wilhelm's rooms so I could protect my bondmate more efficiently. *I suppose I would've been sharing a room if Wilhelm's bondmate had been female.*

I put my pack in the armoire and gently tapped at the door that led to Konner's room. After a few moments, the knob turned, and he opened it a crack.

"What is it?" he asked.

"I'm going to take a walk and get reacquainted. Would you like to come?"

"No, thank you."

I hesitated with my next question, then cleared my throat. "Where will you be?" I expected anger to be the result of my inquiry.

Instead, Konner answered in an understanding and reasonable tone. "I'll remain in the house until you return."

I nodded and left my bedroom. Downstairs, I entered the library. Wilhelm looked up from his schoolwork, and Rowan studiously ignored my presence.

"So how was your reunion with Konner? Did he hug you tightly and welcome you home?" Wilhelm asked.

"Not exactly," I responded.

"Really?" Wilhelm seemed genuinely surprised. "But he —"

"Wilhelm, you better finish your work before Master Todd comes this week, or he'll give you double math again," Rowan cut him off.

"Rowan, may I speak with you for a moment?" I asked politely.

His eyes widened, but he stood and followed me to the entryway at the bottom of the stairs.

"Is there anything I should know from a guardian perspective about this farm or Konner?"

He crossed his defined arms but said, "We aren't that far from the border of Faerie. Vampires do slip in and hunt in this area sometimes. We've been lucky thus far, but we don't usually go out after dark, just in case. It hasn't been easy trying to protect my bondmate and keep watch over Konner, you know," he accused.

Even though you let Konner wander outside alone. I wanted to censure him, but I knew I had no room to complain. "I know. Thank you for watching out for him so far."

"I didn't do it for you," he spat. "He's pretty tough. He even knows some self-defense, which gives him a certain amount of freedom to be outside alone. But I'm glad someone is here to bind with him even if it *is* you. While the house is protected, the farm isn't. With his awakening only five months away, his scent is much more enticing. It may bring nearby vampires here. That would put not only him at risk but Wilhelm as well." He stared at me hard to make sure I understood.

I nodded, and he turned to go back to the library.

"Hey," I stopped him. "Why wasn't Konner bound with someone else? Even with a pup shortage, he would've gotten precedence living in a border town."

His face was an unreadable mask. "You can ask him that yourself." Then he returned to his bondmate.

I exited the house via the front door, passed the chicken coop, and entered the barn. The woody scent of pine shavings tickled my nose as the goats bleated their greetings from their pen. On the left was a large room with workbenches and tables for preparing seeds, seedlings, and drying herbs after they were harvested. Rows of seedlings grew in pots in the warmth of the barn, waiting to be planted.

Konner's parents stood at two workbenches. His father was placing seeds into small pots with dirt, and his mother was speaking spells to some of the seedlings that looked a little droopy.

One of the farm dogs, who protected the plants from herbivores, whimpered from his bed. I beckoned him to me, and he rolled to his back at my feet. His whine made Konner's parents look up.

"Master and Mistress Fireleaf, thank you for allowing me to bind with your son after so many years. I have no excuse for abandoning him, but I'm grateful to be here now." I talked to my feet.

When I glanced up, they'd stood in front of me.

His father gently touched my shoulder. "Glad you could make it, Runa."

"I'm happy to be here, Master Fireleaf."

"Call me Ed, and I was sorry to hear about your parents."

Little Mistress Fireleaf hugged me tightly. "Runa, what a beautiful young woman you've grown into. Now, you don't worry about a thing that happened before today. Konner was pleased to hear you were coming. I don't care how he acts. Just be patient, and he'll come around. I hope you have the same tastes as when you were a little pup because I'm making your favorite for dinner."

"Thank you, Mistress Fireleaf." I smiled at her kindness.

"Oh, call me Kat." Her cheeks dimpled as she returned my smile.

I nodded.

"We scheduled the binding for this weekend. I hope you won't mind a small celebration with just the family?" Ed asked.

"That's perfect. Thank you."

"Well now, why don't you go up to the house and spend some time with Konner? You haven't seen each other in thirteen years," Kat urged as she shooed me from the barn.

I walked back to the house as I was bid but stopped at the front door. Looking to the left, I saw a field of seedlings growing happily under the care of the Fireleaf family. I stared in that direction for a while, looking down the dirt road that led back to town. The wide, open spaces made the wolf inside me want to run, but the guardian wanted to bolt and bar the door.

The farm was so different from the complex I'd left that morning. There was no mansion or outbuildings, no imposing stone walls or hired wolf guards.

My wolf's ear twitched as I got an idea. I entered the house and went to my room.

Removing my clothes, I thought of how long it had been since I'd changed into a wolf. *A couple of months? Too long. Mikhail had so many social functions to attend, and I always had to be in human form.*

I smiled to myself as I imagined the wood floor beneath my paws. It wasn't painful as I willed my spirit into its equally-natural wolf form, like pouring water from one container into another.

I shook myself and trotted happily to the door that went to Konner's room. *This is going to work.* I lifted my paw and scratched at the door.

4

Konner's eyes widened when he found a wolf at his door. I smiled at him and wagged my tail. He tried to keep a straight face, but joy sparkled in his eyes. *Nothing makes people happier than a fuzzy, four-legged friend.*

I nudged his hand with my nose to encourage him to pet me. Once his fingertips touched my fur, he couldn't help himself. He knelt on the floor to have better access. He ran his hands over my head and back, paying special attention to my ears.

After a while, he started to talk. "What beautiful white fur you have. It's so soft. What a pretty girl you are."

I sneezed at him, and he chuckled.

After thoroughly petting me, his hands slowed. "I guess we're going to be bound this weekend," he mumbled.

I couldn't tell if his voice was sad or thoughtful.

I studied him as he stroked me absentmindedly, staring into space. I was pleased my idea to get closer to him had worked, but I wanted to understand his feelings, too.

"Konner, Runa, dinner," Wilhelm called from downstairs.

I realized I hadn't eaten since the night before and found I was famished.

At the sound of his brother's voice, Konner seemed surprised to find himself on the floor petting a wolf. A flush crept onto his cheeks, and he scrambled to his feet. He returned to his room, shutting the door firmly.

I changed into my human form and redressed. Making a quick stop in the bathroom on the way downstairs, I tried to finger-comb my long, white hair where Konner's petting had mussed it. *Get ahold of yourself, you fool,* I told my gray-eyed reflection as she grinned at me in the mirror.

I went downstairs and took the empty seat next to Konner and across from Wilhelm at the dining table.

Wilhelm smiled at me, Rowan scowled, and Konner looked bored and unconcerned. My heart sank, and my idiotic grin twitched into a polite smile.

We passed around the delicious food Kat had made as Wilhelm questioned me relentlessly. What was the Azure's complex like? Was it true they have a mansion? What was it like to live near a city? How did nobles like Mikhail spend their time?

When it started to get really personal, like how did it feel when you were unbound early, Kat interceded.

"Konner, why don't you show Runa around town tomorrow after the chores? I bet there are things she needs to buy. Maybe a new outfit for the binding ceremony?"

"She was just in town today. If she needs to buy something, she can go alone, or Wilhelm and Rowan can take her. You know how Wilhelm enjoys going into town."

"Sorry, Bro. I have to finish my schoolwork before Master Todd comes." Wilhelm winked at me conspiratorially.

"All settled then." Kat smiled.

Konner sighed, defeated.

"Boys, help me with the dishes while Rowan and Runa check the perimeter before dark," Ed said, carrying dirty dishes to the kitchen.

I thanked Kat for dinner and followed Rowan upstairs. We entered our respective rooms, leaving the doors cracked since wolves can't use doorknobs. I removed my clothes and shifted to my wolf state. After nosing the door open, I met Rowan at the bottom of the stairs. His fur was as black as mine was white. His ice-blue eyes watched me impatiently.

Kat opened the front door for us, and we trotted into the pre-dusk light.

With a tilt of his head, Rowan signaled for me to go left. He went right. I investigated the perimeter of the farm, walking around the barn first. I sniffed and listened for scents and sounds that didn't belong. Then I entered the grove. Rowan had marked the edge of our territory, so it was easy to tell where the property line was even in the woods. Somewhere in the middle, I met up with Rowan. We signaled that neither of us had found anything.

As I was turning to head back to the house, I

saw Rowan's ear twitch. I froze to listen. When I hadn't heard anything, I looked back at him. He stared me down with a challenge.

Really? We're going to do this now?

I didn't look away and neither did he. I took in his posture to see how serious he was. His hackles weren't raised. He yipped at me and lowered his front while keeping his back end up.

Playful then.

I pounced on him, but he got away. We rolled and twisted, each trying to get the advantage. We barked and yipped but didn't growl.

Even though we were both earnestly trying to establish dominance, we weren't fighting to injure. We understood there was nothing to gain by doing it that way. The freedom of connecting with another wolf made my heart soar.

Eventually, Rowan pinned me on my belly. I stilled in defeat. Since I had acknowledged his win, he let me up. I took advantage of his relaxed vigilance and managed to pin him.

Evenly matched? I can live with that.

I let him up, and he wagged his tail. Having satisfied his curiosity, he trotted back to the house. I started to chase him, and he ran faster. When we reached the back door, we were both panting, our tongues hanging out.

Rowan scratched the door, and Wilhelm opened it.

"Look at you two. Did you have fun?" He laughed at our wolfy grins.

We went to our rooms to change and redress.

I hadn't had that much fun since I'd been with

Isla. A memory of one of our last days together bubbled to the surface.

"Girls, will you pay attention?" my mother urged worriedly. "You'll be bound next week. I need to make sure you're both ready to be on your own. Do you understand the importance of this rite?"

"Yes," Isla and I said in unison.

"Tell me."

"We must protect the faelings until their awakenings because of the treaty," Isla recited dutifully.

"What is the treaty, and how did it come about?"

"Long ago, werewolves lived in the human realm, but the humans feared us and hunted us until we were almost all gone. The thirteen clan leaders made a treaty with the fae queen for the good of both species. We protect the faelings until they can protect themselves, and the fae make sure the borders of Faerie include werewolf territory to protect us from humans," Isla explained.

"Very good. Runa, tell me about vampires," my mother quizzed.

"Vampires mostly prey on humans since they live in the human realm. But they love fae blood the most. Awakened fae can protect themselves against vampires, but faelings don't have enough magic yet, making them the perfect targets. Sometimes, vampires find a way through the veil into Faerie. Though they mostly come out at night, they have been known to attack in daylight, especially when it's close to the full moon in October. They are very hungry near the Blood Moon."

"Isla, how would you kill a vampire if you were to encounter one?"

"Rip it to pieces."

"Anything else?"

"Cut off its head, stab its heart, or light it on fire and spread the ashes."

"How will you know if there's a vampire around?"

"You can smell them. They smell like wet dirt and bad fruit. Also, they look different. They have fangs, and their eyes glow in the light because of eyeshine." I answered when Isla had been unsure.

"Good, so what can you expect from the bond?"

"Once I'm bound with Mika, I'll be able to feel what he feels, and we'll be able to talk with our minds," Isla answered.

"That's what happens if you're well-matched and in sync," my mother corrected. She smiled at us and knew we couldn't sit still much longer. "All right, take a break before your practical lessons with Seth."

Cheering, we ran out of the drawing room and then the front door. The surrounding land was green lawns dotted with smaller buildings owned by Isla's family. We ran toward the apple tree we loved to climb and reached for the low branches. We sat on a thick branch, dangling our feet.

"We won't see each other after next week," I said quietly, thinking of the future.

"I guess I never thought about it. Your parents won't be my teachers anymore once I'm bound. But what are you going to do after Konner awakens?"

"I don't know. I guess Elva will find me a job."

"Why don't you come work for me?"

"What would I do?"

"I don't know, whatever you want. Do you need a reason to stay with your best friend?"

I grinned at her. "I'll learn something really useful, so you'll have to pay me a lot of money."

She laughed, brushing the cream-colored hair from her yellow eyes. "Deal."

Thirteen years hadn't lessened the ache I felt at the loss of my parents and Isla. Mikhail's parents had told me once that the pain would fade over time, but that hadn't happened yet. I longed for the happy days of my youth when Isla and I were learning to be guardians and running around her family's estate.

A knock at my half-closed door jolted me from my thoughts. I realized I hadn't put pants on yet as Rowan pushed the door open and entered my room. All his earlier hostility was gone after I'd earned his respect as a wolf.

He didn't hide his appraisal of my half-naked body, and I didn't cover myself. As is courteous when an equally-ranked werewolf of the preferred sex evaluates a potential mate, I allowed Rowan to inspect me. I stood still in my shirt and underwear while his ice-blue eyes made me shiver pleasantly, like a lover's cool breath on bare skin.

And I studied him right back. His sturdy jaw

reinforced his alluring combination of shiny black hair and blue eyes. His shoulders were broad and his chest defined. I imagined how firm he would feel under his shirt, and how easily he could lift my weight with his thick arms. My gaze drifted to the front of his pants as I tried to determine how big his manhood was based on his height and girth.

He met my eyes with an appreciative smile, which I returned. "I see guarding the already well-protected hasn't made you lax."

Appraisal over, I pulled my pants on in case anyone else should walk by my opened door. *I still haven't completely grasped the fae sensitivity to nakedness. Of course, I understand why we have to be careful about being naked around faelings, but that doesn't apply to being around Rowan or other werewolves.*

"I trained a lot at the Azure estate."

"Just so, I came to say I was impressed by your abilities out there. I look forward to working with you," Rowan said matter-of-factly.

He extended his arm to me, and I grasped his forearm. I felt relieved to have found solid ground with Rowan. *It'll be much easier to protect Konner and Wilhelm if we can work well together.*

"Well then, now that we're friends, let me give you some encouragement. I know it feels like you and Konner aren't getting along right now but keep trying. He'll come around," Rowan said, heading for the door. "He's in the library in case you're wondering."

Rowan's reassurance raised my spirit. Determined, I went downstairs and found Konner reading at a table in the library.

He looked up to see who was approaching, then returned to his book.

"What are you reading?" I asked, sitting across from him at the table.

"I'm sure you wouldn't be interested." He sighed at the interruption but didn't look up.

"I'm interested in what interests you. Besides, I love to read."

His eyes flicked to mine, surprised, and returned to the page. "I'm reading about humans."

"Really? Fiction or nonfiction?"

"Nonfiction, by Sal Diroot."

"Which one? I've read some of him."

This time, he looked up and maintained eye contact. "*Human Folklore of the Supernatural.*"

"Ah, that's a good one. Have you gotten to the chapter on ghosts yet?"

"No, I'm still on vampires." He paused for a moment, then continued. "I'm amazed at some humans' sympathy for them. Do you think they really believe vampires burst into flame in sunlight?"

"I don't know. But if so, it's probably to make themselves feel safer. I've read that most humans don't even accept the existence of, what they would call, supernatural creatures anymore."

"It's probably better for us if they don't."

"I agree. They certainly can turn violent when faced with the unknown."

He nodded. "What was your favorite chapter?"

I grinned. "I thought the last chapter about aliens was the most fun."

"I have a while before I get to that part."

"What did you think about the chapter on werewolves?"

He pursed his lips in thought. "I was surprised how varied their beliefs are and how they've changed over time. They were much closer to the truth when werewolf territory was in the human realm though they were still way off. Since you all moved to Faerie, their theories have gotten even wilder. A transformation somewhere between a man and a wolf? Ridiculous. No wonder they think it's a curse. But, as wrong as they are about werewolves, what about us? Do they really think we're all tiny women with wings? Pixie dust is pretty funny. Actually, it might be kind of cool to have wings."

"I'm amazed at how imaginative humans are."

He nodded. "It would be awesome to go there one day." He stiffened at his own admission and clamped his mouth shut.

A jolt of fear ran through me at the thought of Konner unprotected around vampires and humans. *He's talking about after he awakens. He'll be able to protect himself then.*

Caution crept into my voice. "Maybe, but it could also be dangerous."

"You think humans would still do you harm?" he asked curiously.

"I think it's a possibility. They seem to have grown as a species, but I can imagine them hunting us down if they viewed us as a threat. I enjoy learning about them, but it's safer for everyone if they believe we don't exist. But, who knows? You're fae, so you can hide your presence with a glamour once you awaken, and you'll have magic to protect yourself. Maybe you'll be a human expert like Master Diroot."

He smiled sadly. "My parents have waited all my life for my awakening so I can help them with the magical aspects of the farm. My mom has already contacted the matchmaker. She hopes my future mate will be the one to guide me through my awakening. I know my parents want me mated soon after so my future mate can help on the farm, too."

I empathized with his sadness at his planned future, recalling what my parents taught me about fae society.

"Have you tried talking to them?"

"There's no use. They've had it all planned out since I was young, and they're very traditional."

"What do *you* want?"

"It doesn't matter."

"It matters to me."

He looked at me, unsure. I stared back sincerely.

"I want to go to a university and learn human studies," he whispered.

"You should tell your parents. I bet they'll understand."

He bit his lower lip and then shook his head. "The farm isn't so bad. I like being here with my parents and brother." He closed the discussion.

"Well, I think you should do whatever makes you happiest."

He nodded thoughtfully, his mussed hair waving as his head moved.

I continued to stare as he looked into space. He'd changed a lot in thirteen years. The last time I'd seen him, he'd been the same height as me. Now, he was a half a head taller than me. He was of a medium build but defined, no doubt from farm work. His round child's face had slimmed down and sharpened. He'd grown out his cowlicked hair to chin-length. The change in length resulted in a pleasantly disheveled look. It was parted on one side, so the front shadowed one eye. His eyes were the only feature that hadn't changed. Depending on how he felt, their brown color could be like rich soil in the warm sun or cold, damp earth in a dark, lonely place.

He cleared his throat uncomfortably when he realized I was staring.

I shifted my eyes to the many shelves of books to give him relief. Scanning the titles, I saw I had read a lot of them. *One benefit of the Azure estate: they have a huge library.*

I hadn't cared much to learn what the future had in store for Mikhail, but I wanted to learn more about the intricacies of fae culture to better understand Konner. I grabbed a book about the awakening ceremony. After sitting back down, I skimmed through the part about unbinding the fae from his or her guardian until I reached information I didn't know.

Once the fae has been unbound, the priest or priestess tells the guide to proceed with the awakening ceremony in a private place.

The magic that has been maturing during the nineteen-year cycle can only be released when the guide and the awakening make a connection. The act of sexual release is not enough to break the seal. The two must trust each other and connect on a deeper level so they can effectively become one.

Interesting. So it's the combination of a physical and emotional connection to an already awakened fae that releases their magic. I know we were always warned that fae sexuality was discouraged before their awakenings because it threatened their magic, but I never knew exactly why. And it's no wonder they push for faelings to find mates rather than use the service if they need an emotional connection for the awakening to be successful. I'm glad I'm not fae. Sure, werewolves don't have magic, but at least we don't have to worry about losing our wolf forms if we have sex. I can't even imagine the pent-up lust.

Peeking back at Konner, he looked like he wanted to say something. I turned my full attention to him to show I was ready to listen, but my effort had the opposite effect. He changed his mind, dropped his gaze to the book, marked the page, and closed it. He rose and returned it to its place on the shelf.

I watched him carefully, trying to determine his next move.

"I'm going to bed," he explained, without looking at me.

I trailed him from the library and up the stairs, taking the book I was reading with me.

"Goodnight," I said as he opened his bedroom door.

He paused and then entered without a response.

I went to my bedroom once I'd determined he wasn't going anywhere else that night. My night vision allowed me to see the furniture without lighting a candle. I placed the book on my desk, removed my pants, and folded them over the back of the desk chair. Then I climbed into the cool, clean sheets in my shirt and underwear. Staring at the ceiling, I thought about what Konner had said and remembered asking my parents about fae society.

My parents' warm hands enveloped mine as we walked down the country road toward my potential bondmate.

"What do you think, Runa?" my father asked as I took in the open fields beside the road. "Do you think you'd like to live on a farm?"

"It's so flat," I observed.

"It is a little different from the mountains and Isla's estate, but after your bondmate awakens, you can return to the pack," my mother reassured.

I nodded solemnly.

"Do you remember how to greet Konner when you meet him?" my father asked.

"Put my hand in his and shake it."

"That's right," he congratulated.

"But why don't fae grasp forearms like we do?"

"Fae and werewolves do a great many things differently because our natures are different. However, our differences are what make the treaty work and keep us both safe," my mother explained.

"Our natures may be different, but the way our societies are built is similar if you really pay atten-tion," my father added.

"Like how?" I asked him doubtfully.

"Well, just like us, fae have traditions and social

norms that dictate acceptable behavior. For instance, you always listen to Elva, don't you?"

I nodded. "She's my alpha."

"Well, fae society is based around filial piety."

"What's that?"

"It's all about respecting your parents and elders, just like you do with us and Elva. They are taught to trust the wisdom of older generations, believing the elders will make decisions with their best interests in mind."

"I trust Elva."

"Right, it's just like that, except it's taught rather than instinct."

I bobbed my head in understanding.

"Fae have a rich and intricate culture. They've managed to embrace the free spirit of magic while maintaining order and upholding tradition," my mother added.

"Oh, okay," I said, not entirely sure what that meant.

"Don't worry, Runa." My mother smiled down at me. "You still have plenty of time to learn. Let's just concentrate on finding you a bondmate. I have a good feeling about the Fireleafs, and they even have a younger son, so you won't be the only wolf."

I increased my pace, eager to meet Konner.

* * *

I sighed loudly into the dark room. *My life so far has been much different than we'd planned. I hope I can earn Konner's forgiveness and make the most of the time we have left together.*

Listening to the sounds of the night, my

breathing gradually slowed as I closed my eyes. A nightingale whistled his rich, powerful song, calling for his mate. Every few minutes, the *hoot, hoot* of the long-eared owl accompanied the nightingale's melody. But it was the constant low croaking of the frogs that helped my mind drift to sleep.

6

The relaxation I felt while falling asleep in a welcoming place was replaced by the usual fitful sleep. It normally took willpower or exhaustion to force me into much-needed unconsciousness.

A rooster crowed his greeting to the dawn, reminding my morning-clouded mind that I was at the Fireleaf farm.

The wooden floor was cold under my bare feet as I jumped out of bed. I knew there were chores to do, so I put on the clothes from the day before, promising myself a good wash and fresh clothes when they were finished.

Opening my bedroom door, I saw Wilhelm leave the bathroom as Rowan entered.

"Good morning, Runa!" Wilhelm greeted. "Seeing your loveliness first thing is more refreshing than morning dew."

Rowan smacked Wilhelm upside his head before closing the door.

"Good morning," I responded, leaning against the wall.

Konner exited his room, hair even messier after sleep.

I smiled. "Good morning," I said to him cheerfully.

He looked up as if taken off guard by my sudden presence. His happily flustered expression seemed to be strangled by something cautious and distant.

"Did you sleep well?" I asked.

Rather than respond to my question, he said, "Meet me in the barn when you're finished."

Rowan came out and patted me on the shoulder when he passed as if he'd heard our conversation and was trying to encourage me.

I used the bathroom quickly and went to the barn. Ed moved fresh fertilizer from the compost pile to the workbenches with a wheelbarrow. Rowan fed one goat while Wilhelm milked the other. The dogs happily ate their breakfasts.

Konner arrived after a few minutes. "We're in charge of the chickens," he explained.

I followed him to the back of the barn where a door led to a storage room with many shelves. He handed me a basket and grabbed a bag of feed. On the way to the coop, he explained what we needed to do.

"I just mixed the bedding, so we don't have to worry about that until next week. When I open the coop door, the chickens will come out. You can go in and collect the eggs, and then take them to my mom so she can make breakfast. I'll feed them, and you can give them water."

We reached the coop, and he unlatched the door.

The chickens were ready to start their day. Some of them approached Konner and pecked at his feet affectionately. Others began digging in the dirt. Once they'd all left, I entered with my basket.

I was prepared to hold my breath, but it ended up being unnecessary. The coop wasn't the most pleasant thing I'd ever smelled, but the primary scents were of pine and herbs. The pine scent was easily explained by the wood shavings used for bedding, but I couldn't identify the herb smells until I approached the first nest to collect the eggs. They were nestled among fresh and dried herbs, primarily lavender and mint.

I collected the eggs and placed them carefully into the basket. Exiting the coop, I saw Konner feeding the chickens as I walked to the house. In the kitchen, Kat was already cooking up a storm.

"Good morning, Runa. How did you sleep?"

"Very well, thank you," I lied, placing the basket of eggs on the counter.

"Wonderful. Breakfast will be done in a bit."

"Thanks." I waved as I left the kitchen.

After returning to the coop, I grabbed the water dishes and walked to the back of the house. I tossed the old water and refilled them with fresh water from the spigot.

Konner had put away the feed and was helping his brother and Rowan clean the goat pen by the time I'd replaced the drinking water in the coop.

When we'd heard Kat call that breakfast was ready, we stopped what we were doing and washed at the spigot. Within a few minutes, we were sitting at the table eating a big, warm breakfast.

As we ate, Kat reminded us to collect our dirty

laundry and deposit it at the back door after breakfast.

Everyone other than Konner seemed happy the two of us were going into town that day. His lack of enthusiasm darkened my mood, and I felt his hesitation in the pit of my stomach.

When we'd finished eating, Konner offered to let me use the bathroom first.

I grabbed my cleanest clothes from my bedroom and went to the bathroom. I didn't know whose soap and shampoo I borrowed, but I vowed to buy some in town to avoid smelling like a man the next day. I was courteous enough not to borrow anyone's toothbrush and just swished water in my mouth. I did, however, use Rowan's hairbrush; his black hair gave it away. *I'm sure he won't mind.* I made sure to clean out my long white hair anyway. *When was the last time he cleaned his brush? He should be thanking me.*

With Konner's help, Wilhelm and Rowan were able to finish their chores early. They were all heading toward the house when I went to fetch Konner.

I felt clean and refreshed with my freshly-scrubbed skin. My long hair was still wet, and I wore a fitted, cap-sleeved shirt, tailored pants with a belt and pouch, and mid-calf boots.

As they approached the house, they noticed me coming toward them. I smiled a greeting, but their responses were unexpected. Konner looked away with an expression that was either anger or frustration. Wilhelm flushed and put his hands in his pockets. Rowan's reaction was the only one I understood. He looked me up and down and smiled, a glint in his eyes.

I sighed inwardly. *No matter how long I'm around fae, I just can't understand them sometimes. Then again, Mikhail's reactions were closest to Konner's. He was usually irritated with me in that long-suffering kind of way. If he ever noticed or said anything about my appearance, it was to criticize and demand that I try harder. "Try harder? Why? I'm a guardian. I'm here to ensure you stay alive. I'm not your doll. My clothes are functional. That is all." The only say he ever had was with my hair. While I felt it was beautiful at this length, it would be far easier to maintain if it was short. Maybe I'll cut it. Is Konner angry because he thinks I should try harder, too?*

Konner walked past me and into the house to take his turn in the bathtub. Wilhelm smiled tightly and mumbled something about schoolwork. I watched him follow his brother inside.

Rowan laughed at their reactions. "Well, you certainly have livened this place up."

I watched the direction in which they'd gone with more than a little confusion.

"What's wrong with them?" I asked Rowan, not wanting to believe Konner's reaction was the same as Mikhail's.

"You've never seen that reaction before?"

"Not exactly."

He considered my answer. Finally, he grinned. "If you don't know, I'm not going to tell you."

I scowled at his teasing.

"On a completely unrelated note, have you attended the Wolf Moon Festival?"

His question surprised me, so it took me a moment to answer. "Yes, this was my second year. Why?"

He shrugged. "I was just curious."

I nodded. "What about you?"

He shook his head. "I never really got the chance. This year was supposed to be my first, but I couldn't get away. It's not like I could leave Wilhelm and Konner unprotected for three days, and there wasn't anyone available to fill in at the time."

"I'm sorry," I felt even worse for Rowan having shouldered my share of the responsibility all this time. *The Wolf Moon Festival is so important for wolves whose faelings are going to awaken soon.*

"I'm glad you're here now. You'll just have to make it up to me."

"What do you have in mind?"

"I'll let you know."

"By next year's festival, Konner will be awakened, and I'll be a full member of wolf society. When they call for fill-ins for the Wolf Moon Festival, I'll volunteer to fill-in for you. That way you can go to the festival. I've been twice and have already met a promising candidate. I can skip so you can attend."

"Maybe, or maybe by next year I won't need to go to the festival."

Even though I'd spent most of my life around fae, I often had trouble understanding their culture, viewpoints, and actions. Werewolves were much more straightforward. Therefore, I knew the implication of Rowan's words and that they were directed at me.

His proposition to get to know each other with potential mating in mind was intriguing, but it didn't demand an immediate response. He let his offer stand as he walked back to the house to catch up with Wilhelm.

7

onner was in the bathroom when I collected my clothes from my bedroom. I grabbed the lot and put them back in my pack. Then I went to the kitchen to drop them by the back door.

Kat was gathering everyone's dirty laundry to take outside for washing.

"Runa, excellent timing," she said as she motioned me to take a sack and follow her to the wash tub outside.

I did as she bid me and dropped the bags where she pointed.

She looked at my pack. "Is that all of your dirty clothes?"

"That's all the clothes I own. I'm sorry, but I left before I got a chance to clean them."

She raised her eyebrows. "That's *all* of your clothes?"

I nodded.

She sucked her teeth in irritation. "Maybe I

should write those Azures a letter and give them a piece of my mind. It isn't as if they don't have enough money to provide you with enough to wear."

"It really wasn't necessary. I was never very interested in clothes and other pretties. In fact, Mikhail always told me to try harder with my appearance. I think my lack of effort embarrassed him."

"But still—"

"Really, Kat, I'm fine. Honestly, I'm grateful to be alive. It doesn't feel right to care about such things when I have so much to be thankful for."

Kat's irritated expression turned sad. She stepped close to me and embraced me tightly. "Runa, I want you to listen to me carefully. What happened to your parents and your friend wasn't your fault. They would all be glad you survived. You're allowed to be happy."

My heart hammered at her words as she forced ugly thoughts into the light. I wanted to believe her, but thirteen years of guilt held me back. "I betrayed Konner. At the time, protecting my dead friend's intended bondmate seemed all I could do for her, but I didn't even do that right. I don't deserve friendship or even pride when I have failed both Konner and Isla." I buried my face in Kat's shoulder, having not felt a motherly embrace in far too long.

"You haven't failed yet," Konner said quietly.

I looked up, my heart racing at his sudden arrival.

"My awakening is five months away. You won't have failed unless I die on your watch."

Kat smiled at her son's attempt to console me.

Her embrace loosened to an arm around my shoulders. "We're counting on you," she encouraged.

I glanced at her, then Konner.

He nodded seriously.

I bowed my head to both of them, promising I'd never fail them again.

Kat told Konner to fetch the money jar from the house. After he was gone, she turned to me. "Runa, I want you to purchase yourself more clothes when you go into town. Get whatever you want. But I have a request: buy one thing that's frivolous but makes you happy."

"But, Kat—"

"No arguing. Please do this for me. I've been trapped here with all men for too long. It'll be refreshing for me to have another girl around. I so wanted a daughter, you know. Just think of it as a welcome home gift."

I nodded. "Thank you."

When Konner had returned, she handed me more than enough money and told us to have fun and be careful.

Within minutes, we were heading down the dirt road toward town.

Konner was silent but seemed thoughtful rather than angry as we walked. It was a long trek, but it wasn't unpleasant that we didn't talk. Konner's words floated in the emptiness that Mikhail had left. *You haven't failed yet.* The hope that Rowan had encouraged felt more possible on that long, quiet hike.

The depot was the first sign we were getting close. Finally, homes and shops lined the streets. The town wasn't nearly as big as the city near the

Azure estate though I didn't really have a preference in town size. I loved both the wide-open spaces and the bustle of a crowd. The company around me was far more important than the location. My eyes drifted toward Konner, and I couldn't fight my smile.

It seemed the middle of the week was a common time for people to go to town. Wagons and carts clattered on the dirt road, causing dust to swirl around the wheels, and bells from shop doors chimed cheerfully as visitors exchanged salutations. Not only were there many people about, but they all seemed to know each other. They greeted each other with smiles and waves. Everyone who passed stared directly at me. *I guess the downside to a small town is that a new arrival is noticed.*

Some people greeted Konner in passing. Finally, one faeling and her guardian were bold enough to ask him about me.

"Konner! I haven't seen you in town for months. Why don't you ever come with Wilhelm?"

"Hello, Chisa. How are you?" Konner greeted the faeling politely.

"I'm berries as always!" She beamed at him, and then she turned her eyes on me as if she'd just noticed my presence. "And who's this, Konner? Did you finally request a guardian? It's about time. It isn't long before your awakening. I'm glad to see you're taking your safety seriously now."

"This is Runa," Konner said reluctantly.

Chisa's smile faltered. Her bondmate, who had been impassive until that point, glared at me with disapproval. Chisa's eager curiosity turned to an air that claimed she couldn't care less. She turned back to Konner as if I didn't exist.

"I wish you good day, Konner." She inclined her head politely and hurried on her way.

Konner met my eyes with a worried expression. "What do you need to buy?"

My surprise turned to shameful misery, but I maintained my composure. "Um, I need to purchase soap, shampoo, a hairbrush, a toothbrush, and some clothes."

"Follow me," he said, watching me carefully.

The people we passed, who'd so recently watched me with curiosity, stared with a range of expressions. Some were like Chisa and ignored me, not sparing even a glance in my direction. Some curled their lips in condemnation, and others glared with malice. I tried to appear unconcerned, but they were really starting to get to me. Instead of worrying about them, I stared at the back of Konner's head as I followed him. His brown waves shone in the sunlight. Hidden hairs of red appeared as if the sun revealed their copper sheen by magic.

They rippled as he looked over his shoulder at me to motion toward an apothecary. We entered the shop, and the prized copper disappeared. Konner signaled for me to take the lead as he didn't know what I wanted. I quickly grabbed a toothbrush and a hairbrush from the easily navigable shelves. They were of a high quality with shiny wood handles and boar bristles.

The shopkeeper appeared from the backroom and gave us a tight smile. "How may I help you?"

"I need shampoo and soap."

"You will want something light smelling so as

not to interfere with your sense of smell while in wolf form, correct?"

I nodded.

She crossed the room to a shelf with many bottles and bars of soap. She reached for a bottle and uncorked it, and then she handed it to me. I put it under my nose and took a deep breath. Its light, woody scent reminded me of running through the meadows of heather with the other pups of my pack. *It smells like home.*

I smiled a teary thanks to the shopkeeper. "I'll take this and the matching soap please."

She nodded. After I'd paid for my purchases, the shopkeeper wrapped them nicely and wished us a good day.

"What kind of clothes are you looking for?" Konner asked as we left the apothecary.

"Ones I can easily move in."

He considered my response, then started to walk. The copper threads reappeared, and I followed them like they would lead me to treasure.

We entered a boutique hidden in the dark corner of a dead-end street. A bell tinkled as we entered the shop. I took in the seemingly chaotic layout of the store. There were colorful clothes and shiny bits of jewelry on every wall and surface. A fae man glanced up from threading purple beads on a string.

"Konner, how have you been? I haven't seen you in a while." He smiled.

Konner gave him a genuine smile, the kind I hadn't seen in thirteen years. My heart leapt to know he was still capable of that smile even if it wasn't for me.

"Hey, Zen, sorry I haven't been by."

Zen nodded his forgiveness, and his eyes slid to me. "I heard some noise about you getting a guardian. I'm Zen." He smiled and held out his hand to me.

I was amazed at his friendliness toward me since everyone else was so distant to the guardian who'd abandoned Konner and returned. I smiled back and shook his extended hand. "It's nice to meet you, Zen. I'm Runa."

"Same here, Runa. But I have to say, in all the times I've heard Konner talk about you, he never mentioned how pretty you are."

Konner's face flushed.

I was shocked to hear Konner had talked about me at all, but I covered my surprise. "Well, he hasn't seen me in a while. I've changed a lot since I was five."

"I'm sure of it." Zen paused to smile again. "So what can I get for you? Are you looking for something specific?"

"I need clothes: loose enough to move comfortably but tight enough that they won't get caught on anything should I need to fight or run."

He nodded his understanding and moved to a basket of shirts. He rummaged through and pulled out a pink top with a scoop neck. It had short sleeves and laced up the front.

I took it from him and held it up. It met all of my requirements and still managed to be pretty.

"Did you make this?" I asked, impressed.

He shook his head. "Everything in here is human-made. I go to the human realm once a month to bring back whatever I think people here will like."

"You go to the human realm? What's it like?"

He smiled at my interest. "It's a lot different from here. If I tried to explain it now, you'd be here for a while. Why don't you finish finding what you need, and we can see how much time we have left? Then I'll tell you all about it."

I shelved my curiosity for later and returned to my task. I dug through the basket from which he'd pulled the pink shirt and found a few other promising choices. Nearby, there was a stack of folded pants. The fabric was blue and had an unusual woven appearance. I ran my fingertips over the top pair to feel the fabric.

"They're called jeans. They're comfortable once you get used to them, and they're sturdy," Zen explained.

Each pair had a tag in the waistband proclaiming a number. "These are sizes? How do I know what size I wear?"

Zen looked me up and down. "You look around a size ten, but you can try anything on in the back."

I looked through the stack of jeans and pulled out the size Zen had suggested. He pointed me to the back of the shop, where there was a curtain in front of a closet-sized space. It made me nervous to have Konner out of my sight in such a public place. When my worried eyes met his from across the store, he seemed to understand and started drifting toward the fitting room.

I'd rather just change clothes here, but that would most likely shock their fae sensitivities. Though Zen has already awakened, so it probably wouldn't bother him.

I closed the curtain of the fitting room and tried the clothes on quickly. Some of the shirts didn't fit but a few did. Zen had suggested the right size jeans. They slid on nicely and buttoned with ease. They hung snugly at my hips and hugged my thighs. They were flexible but durable. I was impressed by the humans' craftsmanship.

I changed back into my original clothes and decided only to get the pink shirt and the jeans. *It'll be nice to have a new outfit for the binding, but I don't really feel comfortable buying more than I need.* I returned the rest of the shirts to their basket.

Moving toward the front counter, a flash of copper caught my eye. I stopped and gazed at a copper key, the same color as Konner's hidden strands. After picking it up from the small table, I turned it over in my hands. The blade was thin and round and ended in a square with a crescent moon cut out of it. The bow was a circle with a seven-pointed star in the center.

"It's made of copper. No iron or silver, so it's safe for both fae and werewolves," Zen informed me when he had seen what I was holding.

"It's beautiful," I commented, already stretching out my hand to return it to the table.

"I have a copper chain too if you want to hang it around your neck."

I examined the key again. Then I remembered what Kat had asked of me. *This counts as something frivolous.*

"All right," I agreed and handed the key to Zen.

I paid for my purchases and was ready to launch into my questions about the human realm. But as Zen handed me the shopping bag, Konner's stomach grumbled loudly. It was lunchtime, and I was hungry, too.

My disappointment at having to feed my stomach rather than my curiosity must've shown on my face because Zen chuckled. "You can always come back another time. Besides, Konner has heard my stories so many times that he can probably tell them better than I."

I waved goodbye to Zen with disappointment, thanking him for his help.

When we had gone outside, Konner looked up at the sky. "Everyone at the farm has probably already eaten lunch. Do you mind eating in town?" he asked.

I shrugged my shoulders and followed him to a nearby café. It was crowded for a small town, but there were still empty tables.

The patrons didn't attempt to disguise their stares.

Konner watched me anxiously. "Are you sure?"

I smiled and nodded my reassurance. *I don't really care how everyone else is acting because Konner is being kind.*

We sat at a corner table and ordered lunch. I blocked out the whispers by playing with the key around my neck.

"Can I ask you something?" I said loud enough for only Konner to hear. When he hadn't responded, I peeked up at him.

He nodded slightly.

"I've been wondering: why didn't you request another bondmate when you'd found out about Mikhail and me?"

His eyes became guarded, and his spine stiffened. I bit my lip, worried he was returning to his cold demeanor. I averted my eyes to the key, readying myself for the lash of his words.

"I didn't want a bondmate who wasn't you," he whispered.

I looked up, surprised, but he was staring at his hands. Everything fell into light: Rowan's initial hostility, Wilhelm's confusion at Konner's cold reception, Kat's assurance that Konner was happy I'd come, Rowan's encouragement that Konner would come around, and Chisa's comment that it was about time Konner took his safety seriously.

I felt a rush of relief and sorrow. "You shouldn't have waited for me," I scolded without bite. "But I'm glad you did."

For the first time in thirteen years, I felt a connection with Konner. I knew we were still well-matched, and we could be a great team that would see him through his awakening.

"I won't leave you until you've successfully awakened. I *will* protect you, Konner," I vowed, promising myself that I'd become worthy of his loyalty and trust.

8

"Can I tell you something?" I asked Konner softly as we walked home.

He dipped his head.

"I should never have been bound with Mikhail. I don't have an excuse, but I want to explain. The night we were bound was the night after my parents and Isla were killed. I couldn't be forced of course, but I was six years old, grief-stricken, and confused. When the adults urged me to bind with Mikhail, I followed their advice. At the time, binding with my best friend's intended bondmate seemed like the only way I could honor her memory and protect who she wanted protected. I felt guilty for breaking my promise to you, but I was desperate to help Isla. I knew your feelings would be hurt, but I thought you'd request another bondmate.

"Once Mikhail and I were bound, it was clear we weren't well-matched. I couldn't find a way to connect with him, and he couldn't or wouldn't forgive me for surviving when Isla had died. By then, it was too late. I tried to make the best of it and be a good bondmate, but he wouldn't let me in. As he got older, he went from resentful to mean. I'm sure I didn't help the situation. I couldn't bring myself to respect him, and he knew that. I just resigned myself to ride out the remainder of my rite with an unworthy bondmate. By that time, I felt so much guilt for abandoning you that I was sure Mikhail was my punishment. I lived a pretty sterile life. I dedicated my time to training and flawlessly carrying out my duties until my rite was complete. My only joys came from reading and, toward the end, leaving the Azure complex once a year for the Wolf Moon Festival. I couldn't believe when Elva had said you didn't have a bondmate, and I was beyond shocked when she'd said you welcomed my return," I finished. "But you already said your parents didn't consult you," I added quietly.

"That's true," he responded, then sighed. "But I'm still sorry I said those harsh words to you when you arrived." He stopped walking and turned to me.

I faced him. His features softened, and he stepped close to me. I let him wrap his arms gently around me, frozen in shock.

"Welcome home, Runa. I missed you while you were away," he whispered in my ear.

I didn't realize I was crying until he pulled back and wiped my tears with his thumbs. I sniffled hard once. "It's good to be home".

He rewarded me with a genuine smile, and I grinned back as I wiped my face with the backs of my hands.

Instead of talking as we started to walk home again, we realigned our relationship to its default settings, effectively pretending the last thirteen years had only been a long vacation.

By the time we'd reached the farm, we were like two childhood friends who hadn't seen each other in a long time and had a lot of catching up to do.

As I headed toward the stairs to put my purchases away, two tall forms burst from the library and landed in a pile at Konner's and my feet. I put myself between the unknown threat and Konner. Then I realized it was Wilhelm and Rowan. They looked up into my confused expression. Without explanation, they lunged at me. I dodged.

"Hey, what—" I started before I had to dodge again.

They both grinned at me with determination.

"You can't beat me, Wilhelm," Rowan said, readying to pounce at me once more.

"Just remember the terms: you have to stay in human form," Wilhelm said, eyes on me.

"Konner, what's happening?" I managed to twist away from them.

I couldn't afford to look at his face, but his voice sounded amused. "It appears to be one of their bets."

"What?"

"My guess is: whoever catches you first wins."

That would explain this behavior at least.

"You boys want to go? Catch me if you can!" I challenged as I ran out the front door, trusting Konner to stay inside.

My unexpected reaction gave me a head-start, but they were close behind. My ability to quickly change direction was the only reason I kept out of reach. When I launched myself into the woods, the chase became a hunt. I quietly moved among the trees, avoiding the sounds of pursuit. I heard a twig snap nearby and hid behind a large tree trunk, peeking around it in the direction of the sound.

"Found you," I heard Rowan say behind me.

I moved to make a run for it, but it was too late. With my first step, Rowan leapt. My only thought was: *if I'm going down, he's coming with me.* My hand latched onto his wrist as he reached forward to tag me. We went down together. He put out his arm to catch himself, and his outstretched hand held the bulk of his weight. The rest slammed into me as he landed on top of me. His abdomen pressed against mine, and it was just as firm as I'd imagined. His solid thigh had spread mine as if making room for him.

"I tagged you first. That means *I* win," I whispered as I grinned up at Rowan, his face not a foot away from mine.

He looked down at me, his ice-blue eyes sparkling. "Are you sure?" He smirked. "Because I kind of feel like I'm winning at the moment."

9

"Whatever game we're playing now, I'm in," Wilhelm interrupted, leaning against the thick tree with his arms crossed.

"I don't think so," Rowan replied seriously, climbing off me. He grabbed my hand and pulled me to my feet.

As we all walked toward the house, I asked, "What did you win in the bet, Rowan?"

He glowed with pride. "Wilhelm has to clean our room and the bathroom for a week."

"Who won?" Konner asked, looking up from his book when we entered the library.

"Who do you think?" Rowan gloated.

"I'm starting to think you lose on purpose, Wilhelm. When was the last time anyone else had to clean the bathroom?" Konner teased.

"Yeah, yeah, enough about that. I want to know what you two were doing out there in the woods." Wilhelm turned the teasing toward Rowan and me.

Konner raised his eyebrows at Wilhelm's suggestive tone.

"Hey now, what happens between wolves isn't for faelings' delicate sensibilities," Rowan non-answered.

A ridiculous image sprung to my mind of Wilhelm's shocked expression as he wandered the Wolf Moon Festival. I laughed aloud, and they all turned to me. "Probably for the best," I snickered.

Our responses seemed to make Konner more curious. "What did I miss?" he questioned his brother.

Wilhelm was pleased to be asked. "Just our wolves getting all snuggly."

"Don't exaggerate, Wilhelm," I chided when I saw Konner's surprise. "He just fell on top of me."

"Fell on top of you, eh? More like you pulled me on top of you," Rowan laughed.

"Well, that's true. I did take you down with me, but where you landed wasn't my fault," I responded matter-of-factly.

Before Rowan could retort, Konner jumped in. "All right you two." He tried for good-natured, but there was an edge to his voice.

I tilted my head at him curiously.

"In any case, I won, and our room really needs to be cleaned." Rowan wrapped his arm around Wilhelm's neck and pulled him from the room.

Konner returned to his book without another word. I picked up the shopping bags I'd abandoned by the front door and climbed the stairs to my room.

After putting my purchases away, I lay on my bed and gazed toward my curtained window.

Rowan's earlier comment and the sun winking through the pale pink curtains brought memories of the most recent Wolf Moon Festival.

The sun winked off the January snow as it played hide and seek behind the clouds. I pulled my cloak tighter to keep the frozen air at bay.

The entrance to the caverns was only a few hundred feet ahead. Wolves from across Faerie shuffled through the cold toward this year's Wolf Moon Festival.

As I entered the cave, I sighed with relief at the warm air that welcomed me. I moved through the crowd of werewolves greeting each other. The tunnel walls glistened as the torches and lanterns illuminated the moist rock.

After a short hike, the tunnel opened into a huge cavern. Stalagmites and stalactites decorated the floor and ceiling and hid entrances to other tunnels and caverns.

I scanned the crowd for any of my packmates. Instead, I found Senry. He met my eyes and smiled a greeting. I gave him a smile and a nod, but I didn't move toward him.

Senry and I had a good time as partners at the previous year's festival, but we'd agreed to meet new people this year.

"Runa!" Kal hugged me from behind.

"Hey, Kal." I smiled and turned to embrace my packmate.

"Have you seen anyone else?" Kal asked.

"Not yet, I just arrived."

"They'll find us. How've you been this last year?"

"Same as always."

"Mikhail still being a jerk?"

I nodded. "How about you?"

"Piper and I are the same mischievous pair." He grinned. "Her parents have started looking for mates for her, and she isn't having it."

"Really? Mikhail seems to be enjoying the matching game."

"Anyway, enough fae stuff. It's time to be wolves! Seen anyone interesting?"

"Not yet, but the festival hasn't really started yet."

"It's never too early," he said wisely.

"What about you? Are you partnering with Oliver again this year?"

He lit up like he thought I'd never ask. "Sweet Ollie and I are to meet in our usual den."

"This is the third year in a row. Do you think you'll be mated once your faelings awaken?"

"I do hope so," he said dreamily. "But it's complicated with the new rules. He isn't sure he can handle it."

"How do you feel?"

"I understand that they're necessary. With vampires attacking not only fae but wolves now, we have to keep the population up. So what? I have to impregnate a female wolf, and then I get to be with Ollie. That's not such a bad deal. Besides, I love pups, and Ollie and I will get to raise at least one of the two we father."

"So then, what's the problem?"

"Ollie isn't sure he can perform for a female wolf, and he feels like he's being unfaithful. But it's for the good of the species. I'll try to convince him."

"You know, I was reading—"

"Yeah, yeah, you and your books."

"Whatever, just listen. I was reading about a way to impregnate without the act of mating. You should look into it."

"Really?" He paused thoughtfully. "I will. Thanks, Runa."

A loud bark echoed through the cavern and drew everyone's attention to the entrance tunnel. The Wolf Council and a group of alphas entered the cavern. Some werewolves around us dropped to their knees at the sight of their alphas. I scanned the group. Elva wasn't among them.

After they had gone down a tunnel toward their separate cavern, I turned back to Kal. "Elva isn't here again this year," I commented.

He shrugged. "She's still young. She won't need to name a successor for a while."

Kal and I walked among the crowd for the next few hours, greeting people we hadn't seen over the last year and looking for our packmates. We eventually found Dai and Mel, but we only smiled and waved as they were already earnestly searching for partners. Then again, their faelings had awakened since the last festival, so they were ready for mates.

When night had fallen, an alpha stood on a large rock and shouted, "Commence with the Wolf Moon Festival!"

"See you later, Runa." Kal gave me a quick squeeze and scurried off to meet Oliver.

I smiled after him and hoped one day to find the love they shared for myself.

The gathered werewolves started to split off into groups, generally by interest. Some began playing instruments while other watched. Some challenged each other to contests of strength or speed. Some went to the cavern where the food was. I watched, fascinated, as one group removed their clothes and shifted. It amazed me they could choose a partner, let alone a mate, in wolf form. I needed to be able to talk to someone first, but that was my preference.

The sexual tension among the crowd built with every minute that passed.

I walked to the cavern where werewolves gathered who had an interest in books and learning. That's what I spent most of my free time doing, so I thought finding a partner with a common interest would be a good idea. Not like Senry; our attraction had been purely physical.

The gathering of werewolves in the cavern I entered was moderate in number. Males and females, all around the same age, talked in loose groups about topics ranging from favorite fiction to history and philosophy.

I drifted from group to group, picking up snippets of conversation as I went.

"Humans are violent creatures who destroy anything they don't understand."

I paused to listen more closely.

"Their murder knows no bounds. They've killed for greed, fear, and mere inconvenience. It's not even survival, either. They turn on each other when there's no one else to satisfy their need to dominate."

Another listening werewolf entered the conversation with a reasonable tone. "Most creatures react violently when they feel threatened. It's true the humans hunted us mercilessly centuries ago, but they've grown since then. At the very least, most don't think werewolves exist. I'm sure we could hide our identities should we decide to go to our realm of origin…"

I drifted on and stopped to listen to two men argue heatedly.

"I don't believe it. It goes against everything we know," the first werewolf said.

"Things change, and it's the only explanation that makes sense. The attacks on pups? The reports of vampire attacks by multiple perpetrators? The vampires are organizing. They're banding together and taking out pups early to leave faelings unprotected," the second werewolf argued.

"That's nonsense. Vampires are nomadic, and they aren't pack hunters. Those reports were probably made up by wolves who couldn't handle a lone vampire. Have you seen them hunt together with your own eyes?"

The second werewolf didn't respond.

"I have," I asserted.

They both turned to me.

"I've seen them hunt together, and he's right. They're targeting pups to leave faelings vulnerable."

"You're lying," the first werewolf accused.

My reasonable tone turned icy. "Excuse me? My parents, my best friend, and her parents were all killed in an attack by multiple vampires. I saw the whole thing, and I was the only survivor. Tell me

I'm lying again, and I'll show you the horrors I've seen."

By the time I'd finished, I was baring my teeth not four inches from his face, and his back was to the wall. He stared at me with wide eyes and didn't say anything.

The second werewolf grabbed my elbow and gently pulled me away. The cornered pup fled for the door.

"You all right?" he asked me, releasing my elbow.

"Fine," I huffed.

"You sure?" He bent to force eye contact.

His amber eyes and fox-brown hair distracted me. I sighed away my anger. "Yeah, I'm fine. Thanks."

He stood to his full height and smiled down at me. "I'm Keir."

"Runa." I grasped his outstretched forearm.

"So then, Runa, would you like to find a free den where we can talk more privately?"

I gave him a small smile and nodded. "I'd like that."

We followed the twists and turns of the cave tunnels and eventually found a free den.

"I'm sorry about your family and your friend," Keir said as he sat next to me.

I nodded. "My friend, Isla, always wanted to come to a Wolf Moon Festival."

"It's too bad she wasn't old enough."

"Even if she had been, she was in the upper class, from a branch of one of the thirteen families. Her parents would've arranged mating meetings with high-class candidates."

"How did you meet her if she wasn't in the same class?"

"My parents were her teachers."

"Ah."

"What about you and your family?"

"We're pretty boring. My father is a civil servant, and my mother is a wolf mystic."

"Really? That's interesting. Any siblings?"

He nodded. "One older sister and two younger brothers. I don't get to see them because I'm with my fae family. But we stay in touch."

"When will your faeling awaken?"

"At the end of this year. Yours?"

"Eight months."

"And what do you plan to do after?"

I shrugged. "I don't have a plan really. I guess I'll ask my alpha to find me a job. What about you?"

"I think I want to become an investigator. I want to discover what the vampires are up to and stop them."

"That's a worthwhile pursuit."

He nodded. "I think so."

We sat in companionable silence for a bit, thinking about the future. I couldn't comprehend a future past Mikhail's awakening. It had been my one goal for so long. It was difficult to see past.

"What about family? Do you see yourself mating and raising pups?" Keir asked.

That's why I'm here, isn't it? No, I'm here to get a break from Mikhail and be around other wolves. And for the physical release, but that goes without saying. "Maybe. I guess I'm not much of a planner. But yes, if I found the right mate. I suppose we all have to do our part for the dwindling pup population."

"That's a worthwhile pursuit," he mimicked me.

"I think so."

We both laughed.

"Well, Runa, would you like to be my partner this year and see how it goes?"

I already felt comfortable with Keir. He was intelligent, driven, and attractive. I gave him a small smile and nodded. "I'd like that."

He smiled as he leaned toward me.

Our lips met tentatively. When we found our bodies reacted, we kissed with purpose.

A year without physical satisfaction from another was, in my opinion, a major sacrifice for guardians.

My hands moved through Keir's fox-brown hair to the back of his neck, pulling him closer with urgency.

He managed to unbutton his pants and remove mine in the time it took me to remove his shirt. Lean muscle stretched across his chest, shoulders, and arms.

As I sat up to remove my shirt, he pulled me onto his lap. Without preamble, he impaled me, his cock finding my core like two magnets drawn together by a natural force.

We both moaned our approval and rocked our hips.

A year seemed to have been too long for us because it wasn't long before I shook with pleasure as he pumped inside me.

We collapsed in one sweaty heap to the blankets on the den floor. Once we'd caught our breath, Keir stretched out on his back, and I snuggled close to his side with my head on his chest.

Three days were spent thus: we talked about a potential future together, and we fucked as if we had to fit in a year's worth, which we did. Sometimes, we would crawl out of our den to eat.

When the fourth day had dawned, we were reluctant to leave the den and return home.

"By next year, both of our faelings will have awakened."

"Mmhmm," I murmured, reaching for him one more time before we had to leave.

"I really like you, Runa. Will you consider me a mate candidate for next year's festival?" he asked as he kissed down my stomach toward my core.

I gasped as he flicked my clit with the tip of his tongue. I wanted to cry yes, but I had to keep my head. I strung my words together one at a time. "If I feel the same way about you next year as I feel now, you will be my only candidate."

I must have answered correctly because he rewarded me by burying his face between my legs.

Longing shook me from my memory. My whole body missed Keir's touch, and I couldn't wait until next year's Wolf Moon Festival. Then I remembered my promise to Rowan that I'd watch Wilhelm for him. *Well, if I still want Keir when the time comes, I'll find a way to contact him. He won't need to go to the festival if he has a mate. But what about Rowan's suggestion that he not go either?*

Our incident in the woods wasn't really enough to topple Keir as the top candidate. *Keir and I have a lot in common, and I would have to wait almost two years before Wilhelm awakens.*

An image of black hair and ice-blue eyes made me question my quick decision. Before my body could heat up any more, Konner called everyone to dinner.

I have time. I put thinking about it away for later.

10

After dinner, Rowan and I searched the farm for signs of vampires and found none. Our work finished, we romped around the yard for a while. It was good exercise and training to play-fight with another wolf, far more useful than my solo training at the Azure estate.

When I'd shifted back to human form and dressed, I heard a knock at my door. I opened it and found Kat.

"Did you keep your promise?" she asked.

I nodded, pulled the key from around my neck, and handed it to her.

She turned it over in her hands. "It's gorgeous," she admired.

"Would you like to see what else I bought?"

"Yes." She nodded enthusiastically, and I invited her into my room.

I returned the money I had left and showed her my purchases. She was particularly pleased by my new jeans.

She smiled as she felt the fabric. "Konner must've taken you to his favorite shop." Her eyes glistened with joy at the thought that Konner and I were friends again.

"So how did you find our little town?"

I opened my mouth to say I liked it, but Chisa's cold shoulder and her bondmate's disapproval stopped me.

"What's wrong? Did something happen?"

"It's fine. Everyone really cares about Konner, so they weren't happy to find out his new guardian was his intended bondmate."

She patted my shoulder. "They just don't understand. They only saw the surface of the issue. Never mind them. Konner wants you here and so do we. Who cares what those busybodies think? It's none of their business."

I nodded. "You're right. I'm glad to be here, too."

We shared a smile before she said, "Well, I better get downstairs for now. Who knows what those men are up to?"

I followed her out and went to find Konner. He was reading in the library. His grumpy mood from earlier seemed to have dissipated. He greeted me warmly with a smile. I grabbed a book that I hadn't read from the shelf and sat across from him. We read for a couple of hours and chatted about our thoughts on what we were reading and related topics. The conversation was interesting, and the mood would've been comfortable and easy were we not so excited to be together again.

When Konner had gone to bed, I was still too wound up. *Maybe a warm cup of tea will help me relax.*

I was startled to find the back door opened until I noticed Rowan sitting on the porch through the screen door. I made a cup of chamomile tea for each of us and went outside.

"Hey, what are you doing out here?" I asked.

He glanced up at me and took the cup I offered. "Just enjoying the night," he said as I sat beside him.

We quietly listened to the frogs, sipping our fragrant tea.

"It looks like you and Konner are getting along better."

"Yeah, I think we've found common ground again. Thanks for the encouragement."

"Anytime." He paused before adding, "It really is a shame you didn't come sooner. It would have been more fun around here growing up."

"I'm sorry to have left you to deal with everything by yourself."

He gave me a slightly embarrassed smile. "I apologize for being so hard on you yesterday. I'm sure you chose to bind with Mikhail for a reason."

"Yeah…it seemed like the right thing to do at the time. Isla really cared about him…You've done an amazing job protecting two faelings alone."

Tugging on his earlobe, he smiled gently. "To be honest, it really wasn't that bad. Konner was always more of the library type, so I never had to worry about him roaming around. And since he refused any other bondmate, it was easy to convince him to learn self-defense. He was a quick study, too."

My eyes widened at his tone. "You were the one who taught him self-defense?"

He grinned. "Of course, my parents run a dojo

after all. They teach pups everything they need to know about protecting fae and fighting vampires before they are bound."

"Wow, I didn't know that…My parents were teachers, too. Well, they were more like private instructors."

He nodded like he already knew.

I wrapped my chilled hands around my warm teacup. "The temperature has really dropped since the sun went down," I commented with a slight shiver.

Rowan gazed over at me, his eyes softening. Then he scooted closer and gently put his arm around my shoulders.

I sighed in relief at his warmth. "Thanks. So are you going to teach at your family's dojo once Wilhelm awakens?" I asked quietly.

"I don't know. Probably. I don't really have a plan other than finding a mate."

I bobbed my head. "I understand the feeling. For so long, I couldn't even imagine a future beyond Mikhail's awakening."

"And now?"

"Now, I'm just trying to find my footing with Konner. I won't fail him again."

His smiled sweetly at me. "You'll be fine."

I returned his smile. "Yeah, I think so, too."

"What's the one thing you'd want to do once you're mated?" he asked curiously.

I laughed. "You mean other than make up for all this chastity?"

He chuckled. "Obviously."

"Hmm, I think I'd like to travel. It might be nice

to be a little wild for a while. You know, enjoy the freedom with my mate."

I felt my face flush when he hadn't said anything. *I've never told anyone that before. Does it sound stupid?*

I peeked over at him self-consciously to find him staring at me intently.

"I feel like you've given me a dream."

My heart jumped at his sincerity.

His ice-blue eyes were cobalt in the dim light that filtered through the screen door. I leaned closer, fascinated by their alluring beauty.

I could feel his breath on my face as we looked into each other's depths.

Just as he began closing the short distance between us, we heard someone descending the stairs.

Regret flashed in his eyes as he pulled away and removed his arm from my shoulders.

I trembled without his warmth wrapped around me, and I wasn't sure it was from the chilly night air.

"What are you two doing out there?" Wilhelm asked through the screen door.

"Having a cup of tea," Rowan answered, taking a sip for emphasis.

I swallowed a cold mouthful in support.

"Well, it's getting late."

"Yeah, we're coming." Rowan stood, and I followed him inside.

After remembering the Wolf Moon Festival and my tension with Rowan, it was a wonder I even got to sleep that night. My erotic dreams didn't provide me with much rest.

11

When morning had come, I mentally slapped myself to remember why I was there.

I half expected Konner to be cold again, but he greeted me in a tired yet friendly tone as we waited for the bathroom.

The next few days were happy and full. We did our chores, laughed, talked, and read together. Everyone else was relieved we were getting along.

The night before we were to finally be bound, we went to bed early. I didn't know why I was so nervous about the following day. But when I finally fell asleep, I relived the night before I had been bound with Mikhail.

Isla and I held hands as the yellow light flashed, and we looked around the depot a few miles from the Azure estate. It was too bad the depot on the estate wasn't finished yet, but we didn't really mind the long walk.

Even though we wanted to protect our faelings, we didn't want to be separated from each other. We had each extracted a dozen promises from the other that we'd stay in touch.

We trudged toward our destination with our parents. I could tell our parents didn't want to let us go, either. If it wasn't for the treaty, we would've had many years together before we left home. They put on brave faces of course, but we all walked with heavy hearts.

We'd traveled about a mile along the dark road, trees twisted as if in agony on either side. I was looking at the moon, struggling to find its way through a fog of clouds, when I smelled it: the smell of damp earth with a nasty sweet undertone. The strength of the odor made me gag. It was much more pungent than I'd imagined.

It took me a second to work out what it was. My breath caught as my heart raced. When my mind caught up, the adults had already shifted; their shredded clothes danced like litter in the cold night wind. By the time Isla and I had shifted, they were close enough to see.

My coiled muscles froze when I saw more than one though the strength of their smell should've been my first clue. Their dark forms moved swiftly among the trees. It was already too late when I realized they were surrounding us. My ears twitched as the adults let out the haunting howls that announced to anyone within earshot that vampires were nearby.

As silence descended, they attacked all at once, outnumbering us three to one.

Their movements were fast as they focused their attacks directly at Isla and me. Though we'd been trained our entire lives for this, our parents guarded us as parents are prone to do. Their initial attacks were rebuffed with growls and the snapping of jaws. They sprang just out of reach, barely escaping our parents glistening teeth. A standoff stilled wolves and vampires alike as we watched each other, calculating next moves.

I had learned the lessons of my parents well, but no amount of classroom description could've prepared me for the sight of an actual vampire trying to tear my throat out.

Their eyes glowed with eyeshine, alight with the recently-arrived moon's glow. Their skin was deathly pale as though the blush of life had never lived there. Their long, sharp fangs looked strange and uncomfortable in their gaping mouths, but capable of tearing flesh none the less. As frightening as all that was, it was their ferocity that made me shiver. They were out for blood, my blood.

Isla's father loosed a snarl and went for the closest vampire's throat. Chaos erupted as furry bodies lunged at the attackers. I tried to take on a number of vampires, but every time I moved to attack one, one of my parents went for it before I could reach it.

A few vampires had been taken out of the fray when I heard it: the crunch of bones and a squeal as a wolf went down. I spared a glance over my shoulder to see Isla's mother, limp and bleeding, on the ground. Isla whimpered next to her, nudging her with her nose. I watched in horror as the vampire that had killed her mother grabbed Isla's father by the throat and snapped his neck with a loud crack, like a stick for the fire. The monster smiled at its triumph as it picked up the helplessly squirming Isla and brought her throat to its hungry fangs. Her body sagged in its arms, and it dropped her lifeless corpse with a too-quiet thump.

My throat burned as I howled in sorrow and rage. I rushed toward my best friend's murderer. Before I could launch my attack, I was snatched up by the back.

My mother clutched me in her mouth as she had many times when I was very young. My legs dangled under me, and I tucked them in since I was too big to be carried that way. As she ran toward the Azure estate, I saw the full scope of the carnage. Isla and her parents were splattered all over the road. Their blood dripped, splashed, and leaked like a macabre painting. My father was covering our escape when they pounced on him, ripping and tearing at him as he snarled, then went silent. The werewolves I'd loved my entire life had become someone's dinner in a matter of minutes.

My mother's breath was hot in my fur as she ran from the remaining vampires, who pursued us until we got closer to the complex.

She managed to get inside the gates and shift before I realized she was injured. She clutched me to her chest as fae and werewolves rushed to help her. The gash in her stomach seeped blood into my fur.

"Vampires...in a...pack," my mother told anyone who was listening. "Runa." She grabbed my face and forced me to look at her. "My daughter, you're safe. Mommy loves you, Runa."

As she sighed her last breath, I howled myself hoarse in agony at my loss.

I realized I was howling in my sleep as Konner tried to calm me in the dark. "Runa, it's a nightmare," he hushed.

My howl turned into a whimper. My clothes lay in shreds on my bed from when I had shifted in my sleep. Konner knelt beside my bed, petting my head and stroking my ears until I was calm. I slowly drifted in and out of sleep.

When I had awoken, I saw Konner dozing, slumped against my bed. His eyes fluttered open when I shifted my weight.

"Are you all right now?" he asked, stretching his back and limbs.

I nuzzled his chin and licked his face to tell him I was fine and to thank him.

He laughed and petted my head again. When he realized why I couldn't shift back with him in the room, he flushed and returned to his own room.

As I shifted and dressed, I gave every movement more concentration than it warranted, forcing the nightmare to fade into distant memory where it belonged.

12

*A*fter the usual chores, I bathed and dressed in my pink lace-up top and jeans. My key necklace hung around my neck in its customary place.

There was a lot to do before the fae priestess and wolf mystic arrived to bind Konner and me. Kat wanted me to help her in the kitchen. But when I'd explained I was a lousy cook, Konner switched tasks with me. I was content to dust and polish the house instead.

After lunch, the clergy arrived to prepare the space for the binding ceremony. Ed showed them where the ceremony would be held. As evening approached, they announced they were ready for us, and we all walked to the spring.

The fae priestess began. "I call forth Konner Fireleaf."

Konner stepped forward.

"Konner, do you enter this bond freely and with an open heart?" she asked.

"Yes," Konner responded.

"I call forth Runa of the Mountain Meadows Pack," the wolf mystic said, and I stepped forward. "Runa, do you enter this bond freely and with an open heart?" he asked.

"Yes," I answered.

They motioned for us to join hands and look at one another. I stared into Konner's warm brown eyes as the wolf mystic addressed me.

"Runa, do you swear to protect Konner from every threat until you are unbound at his awakening?"

"I so swear."

"Konner," the fae priestess said. "Do you swear to trust Runa and not take advantage of her oath to you?"

"I so swear."

Together they pronounced, "From this moment, until the day of unbinding, you are bound together. Two minds of one mind, two hearts of one heart, and two spirits of one spirit. So it is and so it will be."

The emptiness Mikhail had left filled in a golden rush with Konner. A tether formed between our hearts. I welcomed the comfort and bliss that comes from protecting someone you care about, and for the first time, I felt Konner's emotions. Heat radiated from my chest to my limbs as I sensed his fulfillment, satisfaction, and joy.

When he smiled back at me, I knew he perceived my emotions, too.

After the ceremony, the clergy stayed for a celebratory feast. Konner turned out to be a much better cook than I. As dusk approached, they took their leave.

Rowan and I checked the perimeter. I was so happy that our playful training was more play than training. As I romped around the yard with Rowan, my stomach quivered when Konner's unease trickled through the bond. I rushed toward the house to see what was wrong. But, when I got there, Konner was reading in the library. I shifted and dressed, then met him there.

"What's wrong?" I asked, sitting across from him.

"Nothing," he answered. As he smiled at me, the unease from before disappeared.

I guess the bond will just take some getting used to.

"Remember when Zen said you know his stories better than he does? Will you tell me about the human realm?" I was interested in the human realm, but I also thought listening to Konner talk for a while would help me decipher his inner voice.

As expected, his excitement hummed through the bond. I found it affected me as anticipation rushing through me.

"The first thing Zen always talks about is how many humans there are. There are billions of them! Isn't that incredible? They live in cities and towns and in the country like us, but they get around in automobiles, trains, and airplanes."

"I read a Diroot book about human transportation. It amazed me. Why don't they use transportation circles? It's so much faster."

"They can't use magic."

"They can't, or they don't know how?"

"I'm not sure."

"What else?"

"They can talk to each other over long distances using a telephone."

"What's that?"

"I don't know exactly how it works, but it transmits your voice through a device to another device at the desired location where the other person can hear you. They can do the same thing with images. That's called television. They don't use candlelight to see after dark but have a power called electricity that feeds energy to many of their devices."

"It sounds like magic to me."

"That's what I said, but Zen said they don't believe in magic anymore. They believe in something called science."

"What else does electricity power besides light?"

"Everything. They have stoves that don't use wood and can provide heat without fire. But the most amazing device Zen told me about is called a computer. It's like a magic box that has every book in every library, and it can fit on a desk or in your hand. You can even use it as a telephone or television."

"I would love to have something like that. The humans seem to have many wondrous things."

His heart was full of longing and hope as well as crushing sadness and regret.

I tried to distract him. "What else?"

He told me so much more about their technology, how they live, some of their customs, their geography, their history, everything he knew. We talked late into the night. He knew so much but insisted it was a drop of water in a rainstorm compared to what he didn't know. When it had long been past time for bed, we said goodnight and went to our rooms.

I don't know if it was lingering feelings of failure, fear of the unknown, or if my mind had indigestion, but my dreams that night were a medley of memories of my time with Mikhail.

Everyone steered clear of Mikhail as he strutted down the street.

A young fae street urchin burst from a side alley. He narrowly missed knocking into Mikhail and slammed into me. I steadied him before he fell.

"Are you all right?" I asked, looking down at him.

"I'm sorry, Miss." He quivered, peering down the alley.

"Don't worry about it. What's wrong? Is someone after you?"

Mikhail sneered at us and tapped his foot.

"I thought I saw a vampire," the boy whispered, shaken.

"Where's your bondmate?" I asked.

"I don't have one. I don't even have a home to support one."

"What about you parents?"

"Gone."

I knelt so I was at eye level with him. "You know, there are programs for fae like you. Werewolf families take in faelings without homes or families."

Mikhail's impatience was turning into anger as he realized what I was going to do.

"Come on. Let's get you to Faeling Affairs. They'll take care of you. All right?"

He squeezed my hand as we walked.

Mikhail followed close behind, his anger mounting with every step. After I'd said goodbye to the young faeling, Mikhail loosed his fury on me.

"My entire schedule is ruined because you feel it necessary to help every filthy thing you come upon…"

…I scrubbed my face and hands and put on my nicest outfit. Mikhail was going to meet potential mates at this party, and I didn't want to mess anything up for him.

I met him outside the complex's depot. He looked me up and down, then curled his upper lip.

"You couldn't have tried more, Runa? You scream low-class. If you screw this up for me, I will never forgive you…"

…I didn't know Mikhail's friends were visiting today. I entered the salon as they were sitting for tea. The two boys rose from their seats as I approached. Mikhail flushed in embarrassment at my presence but introduced us.

"Runa, these are my friends, Thomas and Frederick. Frederick, Thomas, my new bondmate, Runa."

Frederick was closer to me and held out his hand. I grasped his hand and shook it. "Nice to meet you." I smiled.

All three boys' mouths hung open, looking scandalized. Mikhail turned crimson with humiliation and anger.

Thomas recovered first and reached for my hand. He took it gently in his and bent over it, showing me how a proper high-class greeting went...

...Thomas's and Frederick's bondmates and I kept a respectful distance as the young men drank tea at a fancy café.

"You're exaggerating," Thomas said to Mikhail.

"I am not," Mikhail defended. "She is insufferable. She is low-class in every way. She does not even care about her appearance. Isla was so beautiful, graceful, and outgoing. I think Runa looks and acts like a common mutt just to embarrass me. I am almost grateful she is so introverted. At least she does not broadcast her inferior quality."

My limbs felt too heavy to move as my mind resurfaced into the waking morn. After what had seemed like a half hour of wrestling, I cracked my eyelids. My blurry morning vision focused on Konner's brown eyes staring into mine as he lay beside me.

Neither of us spoke. I knew he must have seen my dreams by the tenderness in his eyes. He reached out and covered my hand with his.

"I will never hurt you, Runa," Konner whispered.

"I know," I murmured.

We lay quietly for a while, his comfort burying the bitterness of my memories of Mikhail.

A knock on Konner's door in the adjacent room made him jump from my bed in a panic.

I shook myself to return to a normal mindset. *It's one thing to be friendly with your bondmate, but I don't think even Kat and Ed would tolerate Konner and me in the same bed. Even if we weren't doing anything, it's much too close to the taboo of fae and werewolf matings. Maybe it would be different if we'd grown up together, but that isn't the case. I need to do a better job of shielding my mind so Konner doesn't see my dreams. I mean, who knows what my unconscious mind will come up with next?*

Still, I was warmed by the image of Konner's dark hair caressing his face and the tips of his pointed ears peeking out from the tousled waves.

13

It took a couple of weeks before Konner and I got the hang of feeling each other emotions. By then, I felt I truly belonged at the Fireleaf farm. Konner and I enjoyed being around each other. We read together and talked about everything that interested us. He told me more of Zen's human stories, but he didn't talk about wanting to go to a university again. The Konner who was cold and distant, the one who'd greeted me on my arrival, became a memory. He returned to the kind, caring, curious Konner who wanted to share everything with me for the price of a smile.

Rowan became a good friend and playmate. He kept me connected to my identity as a wolf. Our nightly romps made both of us better guardians. Rowan was like the wind. He was at my back when I needed a push or slowing my steps when I needed to stop and think. He was a breath of fresh air that brought scents from faraway places I had yet to experience. He could be as gentle as a breeze that carries a falling feather or as fierce as a gale that makes sailors pray for port. He was a wind that blew from somewhere unknown and beckoned me to follow it to whatever mysterious place it was going next.

Wilhelm was the same as always: light-hearted and funny. He continued to tease everyone good-naturedly and lose bets to Rowan. He never begrudged a laugh at his expense but instead would laugh with everyone else. He quickly became like a younger brother.

Every few days, Kat and I would have some girl time. Sometimes we'd talk about the future. She hoped for grandchildren soon after Konner's awakening. She asked me how many pups I wanted after my fertility was restored during the unbinding ceremony. She asked if I had any mate candidates, and I told her about Keir. Other times, we'd sit on the floor as she brushed my hair, which she was decidedly against me cutting. She became more like a friend than a mother though she did have words of wisdom for a happily mated life.

Ed was a strong, quiet presence. We didn't talk a lot when we were alone together but just enjoyed the quiet. I found it comforting to be around him.

One evening at dinner, Kat turned to Konner seriously. "You'll have a visitor tomorrow, Konner."

Konner immediately tensed for impact, and my chest tingled with his dread at what she would say next.

"The matchmaker is sending over a potential mate. Her name is Raina."

As Konner nodded, wearing a complacent mask, his heart was not so calm. I could feel he was a jumble of warring emotions. But as my stomach dropped out and I started to go numb, I knew the winner was hopelessness. I veiled my expression as well though I wanted to jump in and protect him. He wanted to awaken, but mating represented saying goodbye to his unexpressed dream.

"When is she coming?" Konner asked diplomatically.

"Midmorning. You should have time to take care of your chores and clean up before she arrives."

His nod was reminiscent of a stamp that sealed his fate.

That evening, we went to the library as usual. But instead of reading, Konner stood at the window and stared into the night.

I didn't urge him to tell his parents what he truly wanted. I didn't have to. I felt helpless as I couldn't protect him in this situation. Instead, I wrapped my arms around his torso from behind, resting my cheek on his back. I tried to send comfort through the bond. It didn't dissipate his sadness, but it wrapped him in the warmth of someone who cared he was in pain.

"I'm sorry you're hurting," I whispered.

Wanting me not to suffer with him, he lied to me. "It's fine. I'm sure everything will work out just fine."

His lie didn't convince either of us.

"I suppose I should go to sleep. I better look rested for my potential mate." He walked out of my embrace. Glancing over his shoulder, he smiled softly back at me. "Goodnight, Runa."

Konner's apprehension kept me from falling

asleep. Feeling like I needed to check on him, I crept into his room to see if he was still awake.

His bedroom was set up like mine, but it had more of a Konner feel. His scent filled my nose. It was potent and earthy with a combination of sweet and spicy undertones.

Konner lay on his bed, absently staring at the flame of a candle on the bedside table. His eyes shifted to me as I approached. I sat beside him and smiled gently.

"Are you having trouble sleeping?" I whispered.

He shrugged.

"I wish there was something I could do for you."

His eyes widened.

"I don't want to be alone right now." Konner's voice echoed in my mind through the bond.

I gasped when I'd realized our bond had reached the telepathy stage, then smiled.

"I'll stay until you fall asleep."

He nodded and shifted his position to lie on his back, but my stomach was still clenched with his anxiety.

In the dim light from the candle, I could see rectangles of glossy paper pasted to the walls. Each paper had what looked like realistic drawings of people, landscapes, buildings, or objects.

"What are those?" I asked, staring at them.

"Postcards and photographs. Zen brings them back from the human realm. Remember when I told you about cameras? These are the resulting images."

"They're beautiful."

He smiled softly.

After looking at his collection for a while, I realized Konner was staring at me rather than trying to go to sleep.

"*Well, go ahead. Go to sleep. Is the candle keeping you awake? Should I blow it out?*"

"*I don't want to quite yet.*"

I sighed. "*If you aren't even going to try to sleep, I'm going back.*"

I stood to leave, but Konner stopped me by grabbing my hand. I glanced back at his pleading eyes and sighed.

After motioning for him to move over, I laid down beside him on top of the blanket. "*Go to sleep.*"

His hair was feather soft when I reached out and stroked it. He watched me in the dim light for a while before the sensation made his eyelids heavy.

As soon as his breathing slowed, I blew out the candle and returned to my bedroom.

14

When I went outside for chores the next morning, Konner was still tense, not ready to face a potential mate.

"How can I help?" I asked through the bond as we tended to the chickens.

"Stay close," he pleaded.

"You got it."

After our chores had been finished, we washed up to look nice for our guest. When I entered the library, I saw Konner gazing out the window again. I felt a little sick as I took him in. He wore slim black pants, a white collared shirt with the top two buttons undone, and a hip-length navy jacket with wide notched lapels and cuffed sleeves. The sunlight streaming through the window revealed the strands of copper in his brown waves.

I ran my fingertip along the blade of the copper key around my neck.

His shoulders and back stiffened as he no doubt felt what I was feeling as I looked at him. His eyes slid to mine. If I hadn't known better, I would've said he was daring me.

Wilhelm stuck his head into the library. "Heads up, Rowan said he saw a carriage stop outside."

Konner nodded his acknowledgement. *"Stay close,"* he implored.

I dipped my head.

Kat and Ed were gracious as they answered the door to welcome Konner's potential mate. They showed her to the parlor, then left the room.

Raina entered, trailed by a wiry fae man. She was tall and held her head high. Her expression was calm, neither pleased nor displeased. Her brown hair was pulled up, and her dress looked expensive.

Konner stood to greet her, offering his hand. "It's a pleasure to meet you, Raina," he said, shaking her hand.

Her calm mask frowned ever so slightly at the gesture. "Of course." She replied like her presence was a gift. The fae who accompanied her helped her into a seat and stepped back to wait behind her chair should she need anything.

Kat and Ed returned from the kitchen, bringing tea. Kat set the tea tray on the low table and sat beside Konner. Ed sat in a chair nearby.

Raina's escort prepared her tea and handed her the cup and saucer. She brought the cup to her lips as if to drink and delicately sniffed the brew. Then she set the cup back in the saucer without tasting it.

I hovered in the background, tensing at her rudeness.

"So, Raina, the matchmaker tells me you are very accomplished." Kat tried to ease the tension through conversation.

"Yes." Raina didn't elaborate but looked around the room critically.

Kat tried again. "I hear you are particularly gifted at helping plants grow. What type of plants do you enjoy working with?"

"I excel at flower arranging. I breathe new life into plants that are already clipped."

"We primarily work with living plants in soil," Kat explained.

"Yes, I do not do dirt."

Another tense silence suffocated the room.

"So you awakened last summer?" Kat continued into the void.

"The summer before."

Kat crinkled her brow, surprised she'd been misinformed.

"I have high standards," Raina said by way of explanation.

"Well, it's always admirable to know what you want. Our Konner is quite the match. He's well-read and can already perform a little magic before awakening."

Raina stared at Konner doubtfully. "What kind of magic?"

"I can cast a decent glamour," Konner admitted.

Raina was unimpressed. "Not terribly useful unless you are going to the human realm, and why would anyone want to do that?"

"You aren't interested in humans?" Konner asked.

Seeing that Konner and Raina could continue their conversation without help, Kat and Ed excused themselves from the room.

Raina's eyes squinted, and she curled her upper

lip like she'd stepped in something nasty. "They are uncouth children with no magical abilities and little to no knowledge of the world around them."

Konner clamped down on whatever retort was about to burst from his mouth. He twitched in irritation but let silence reign.

"Tell me, Konner, what do you plan on doing once you awaken?" Raina interrogated.

"My parents would like me and my mate to help with the farm."

She nodded. "That is understandable. And what help is expected? Distribution? Sales perhaps?"

Konner inclined his head at her question. "Distribution and marketing are handled by my mother's family. We will just be working on the farm: growing and harvesting."

Her frown was deeper this time. "Leave us," she demanded of her attendant, who promptly left the room. Her eyes shifted to me, and she raised her eyebrows. "Well?"

Konner jumped up with indignation. "Runa is not a servant. She can stay if she pleases."

I stood my ground.

Raina squinted at me. Then she turned back to Konner. "It seems to me there has been some mistake. I cannot comprehend why we were matched. We are not even in the same class."

My body flushed as anger flooded the bond when Konner heard her tone. "The matchmaker is aware of our financial and social status. We are in the same class."

"You are a *farmer*. I am a *merchant*. Just look at this place. You seriously cannot expect me to live here and play in the *dirt*."

Konner's fury was beyond words. Before he could collect himself to say something really rude, which she no doubt deserved, I stepped in.

"Raina, was it? I believe this meeting is over. Please return to your home safely and give our regards to your family." I led her by the elbow, escorting her to the door.

Her attendant scrambled down the front stairs to catch up with her, and I slammed the door behind him.

Both Konner and I shuddered in ire. But as I turned to face him, the feeling dissipated. We sighed in mutual relief.

"There's no way my parents will want me to mate her."

I smiled up at him. *"I'm happy for you, Konner."*

Disaster averted, Konner and I returned cheerfully to the library to read and converse.

Everyone was horrified as we related Raina's behavior at dinner that night.

"I'm going to have a serious discussion with that matchmaker," Kat asserted, displeased.

15

That evening, I had more energy to burn than normal. My play session with Rowan got a little rough. After we'd come inside and returned to our rooms to shift, I heard a knock on the door leading from my room to Wilhelm and Rowan's room.

That's unusual. Normally, Rowan uses the hall door if he wants to talk. I opened the door, and he kicked it closed behind him as he rushed me. He grabbed my shoulders and spun me around, pinning me to the door. My gasp was replaced by a soft moan as Rowan crushed my mouth with his and pressed his solid body against mine.

I had enough presence of mind to wonder if my roughhousing that night was what encouraged Rowan to act but not enough to fight the heat building in my core. I slipped my tongue into his mouth and ran my fingers through his lush, black hair.

At first, I thought the slight sickness in my

stomach was my positive sexual reaction to Rowan. But then, the pleasant feeling turned into an intense nausea and was followed by heart-wrenching despair. I heard Konner's voice in my head, *"Stop it, Runa!"*

The intense emotions through the bond shriveled my arousal, and I pushed Rowan away. His hurt expression at being rejected was a fraction of the agony expressed on Konner's face as he watched from the hall door.

Rowan followed my eyes over his shoulder and saw Konner. Rowan cursed under his breath and ran his hands through his hair. As we stared, Konner fled. I glanced at Rowan, and he waved his hand, telling me to follow Konner. I ran for the door.

"Wait!" Rowan called before I reached the hallway. I looked back, and he held out my pants, which I hadn't yet put on after shifting. I snatched the pants, stuffed my legs into them, and pursued Konner without worrying about shoes.

I opened Konner's bedroom door, but he wasn't there. I checked the library and the parlor. He was nowhere in sight. My heart pounded in my tight chest when I couldn't find him in the house at all. Trying to calm myself enough to feel where he was, I followed the tether from my heart to his. My mind froze, horror-struck, when I realized he was outside. I stood at the back door and stared into the darkness, trying to locate him. When I discovered what direction he was in, I didn't hesitate. I opened the door and stepped into the night.

"Konner!" I called over and over through the bond, but I received no reply.

I moved swiftly and quietly through the woods toward the spring, ears and nose pricked for anything vampire-like.

"Konner, please!"

I finally found him, crumpled on the smooth rock at the bank of the spring.

"Konner," I whispered urgently. "Please come inside."

He didn't respond.

I crept toward him and reached for him.

"Please don't," he demanded before my outstretched hand reached him.

I let it drop to my side.

"Don't touch me with the hand that just clung to Rowan," he spat.

"Konner—"

"I'm sorry, Runa. I just…" He paused as if choosing his words carefully. "I just got you back. I've waited for so long, and I didn't want to share you even with Rowan. But I'm still sorry. I'm being selfish. Of course, you're thinking about what you want after I awaken. It just took me by surprise. Really, I want what's best for you. I won't stop you from being with Rowan." His voice sounded reasonable, but I could still feel his pain.

"I wasn't thinking of the future. At the moment, I don't yet plan on mating Rowan. That was just my body's natural reaction. But if my being with Rowan upsets you, I don't have to be. All guardians know they may have to be chaste for most of the year. Seeing you through your awakening is still the most important."

My chest was hollow with Konner's misery. I couldn't tell the exact reason for it, but the emotion was clear. He sat, wallowing in the dark with his back still turned toward me.

I reached for him again, and this time he didn't stop me. I stroked his hair in a soothing gesture. *"Can we please go inside?"* I pleaded.

He stood stiffly in response.

I grabbed his hand, and we ran to the house. Kat and Ed must have already gone to bed because only Rowan waited nervously by the back door.

"Konner, could you give us a minute?" I asked.

He nodded, reluctantly released my hand, and left Rowan and me in the kitchen.

Once alone, Rowan stepped closer and asked in a low voice, "Is he all right?"

I shook my head. "I think we really shocked and upset him."

"Yeah, well, fae are like that. He'll get used to it." He opened his arms, inviting me into his embrace.

I gazed up into his eyes and shook my head. "It's not a good idea right now, Rowan."

"I don't understand why he's so upset. It isn't as though he's a possible mate for you. He knows it's forbidden for fae and werewolves to mate."

"You're right. I don't think that's what it is. I think he just wants what little time we have left together all to himself. I think he's feeling vulnerable. Because I left him once before, I think he's afraid you'll take me away."

Rowan seemed unconvinced and more than a little disappointed.

"Hey, you know what being a guardian entails. They come first." I tried to soothe the rejection.

"Yeah, I know."

"Besides, it's not like we won't see each other every day, and we still have months together. Potential matings aren't all about sex, you know."

"Easy for you to say, you've been to the Wolf Moon Festival before," he mumbled, pouting.

"You'll have plenty of time in the future."

"With you?"

I laughed at his incorrigibility. "It's possible."

He grinned suggestively. "Something to work toward."

"Sure, go with that. Everyone has to have goals."

"You're going to want me so hard by the time Konner awakens. You'll beg for me to take you."

"You sure are confident."

"Because I've seen your reaction to me."

"But you haven't seen my reaction to Keir."

"It doesn't matter. We're already friends and a good team. Why would you choose someone you barely know?"

"That's a good point. However, Keir's faeling will awaken by the end of the year. Wilhelm is still a few years off. What do you suggest I do until then?"

He bit his lower lip at that logic. Finally, he gazed deep into my eyes. "I'm worth the wait," he said seriously.

Rowan is right about my physical reaction to him and the fact that I know him better than Keir, and we are already friends. But, just like with Keir, I have no deep feelings that I'd call love, at least not yet. Of course, love isn't the only reason to mate someone. It's not even the most important reason.

I stared back at Rowan with real consideration. "I know you are."

16

When I'd returned to my room that night, I knocked gently on the door to Konner's room. He opened it but wouldn't make eye contact.

"I talked to Rowan. He understands the rules. It's just you and me until you awaken." I thought the news would brighten his mood, but he was still miserable. I looked around helplessly. "What else can I do, Konner?"

"Nothing," he said. "This whole thing just makes me realize what little time we have left. Then you will be gone again."

I understood his grief. "I'm sorry. It's my fault we don't have more time."

"No, Runa. That's not—"

"It's the truth. But we can still be friends after. We just won't see each other as much."

We both stood in silence as the loneliness of the future settled on top of us.

"We should probably go to bed," I whispered after a while.

Konner reached out and pulled me into an embrace. Resting my cheek on his chest, I wrapped my arms around him in an attempt to ease the ache in my heart.

"Stay with me tonight," he pleaded through the bond.

I pulled back and gazed into his eyes. They were ready to shatter. I nodded slightly, and he gave me a broken smile.

He led me by the hand to his bed. My eyes flicked worriedly toward the door. *Even though I know nothing sexual will happen, I don't want anyone to see us sleeping beside one another.*

Konner caught the gesture and locked the hall door. As we settled under the blankets, I made sure to keep space between us.

We stared at each other in the candlelight. My proximity and the feeling of my hand in his soon calmed Konner enough for him to fall asleep.

Watching him breathe slowly and steadily as the copper strands of his hair danced in the candlelight soothed me until I couldn't keep my eyes open.

That was the first night I spent in Konner's dreams. They were all over the place and started with reliving a memory from the day after I'd arrived.

I'd just finished helping Wilhelm and Rowan with the goats, and we were walking to the house to clean up.

Runa exited the front door and smiled warmly at me. Her face was flushed from a recent bath, and her long, wet hair clung to her face and neck. One drop of water trailed from her collarbone and disappeared into her shirt

My cock stiffened and pressed painfully against my pants. I couldn't ignore the warm and tingly sensation that traveled down my shaft as I imagined following that drop of warm bath water.

I wrestled with my desire, frustrated by my lack of control. I strode past her without a word. *Get a grip, Konner. You're losing it. It's not worth your magic…*

…I headed up the stairs to Runa's room to tell her I'd just finished the Diroot book on human views of the supernatural. The door was partially opened, so I looked inside, lifting my hand to knock. Instead, my hand covered my mouth to muffle the gasp that escaped.

Rowan pressed Runa roughly against the door that connected their rooms. One of his hands stretched out to the door behind her. The other wrapped around her waist, trapping her in his embrace.

I pushed the door open to stop him from assaulting her. Then I saw the rest. Runa's hands swam in Rowan's black hair as she pulled him even closer.

Bile burned my throat while I watched them enjoy each other. *"Stop it, Runa!"* I screamed in my mind as my heart felt like it was being ripped from my chest.

Runa pushed Rowan away and stared directly at me…

…I lay in my bed half awake. In the dark, I

heard the turn of a doorknob and the soft padding of bare feet on the wood floor.

"What—"

"Shhh," Runa hushed me. Then she lifted the covers and climbed into my bed. She snuggled close to me. "Konner," she whispered in my ear. "I want you."

"I thought you and Rowan—"

"Forget Rowan. It's just you and me."

"But if I connect with someone physically and emotionally before my awakening, I'll lose my magic."

She grabbed my hand and brought it to her breast. "It'll be worth it," she breathed hot in my ear.

The warm, squishy weight in my palm made my balls tighten in anticipation. I flexed my fingers, and she moaned softly…

***

I was ripped from his fantasy as Konner squeezed my breast in the real world.

He was still asleep when I scrambled off the bed.

It was early morning; the sun had not yet risen. I sat in the dark while my mind ran amok.

Konner wants me? I don't understand. He'd even give up his magic? But fae and werewolf matings are forbidden, the most forbidden in fact, in order to preserve species purity. We'd both be outcasts. How could he even consider it?

Then I looked at Konner's sleeping form. His dark waves fell into his face. I had the sudden desire to brush his hair away so I could gaze upon him. I fought the urge. Then I thought about his tall, strong body under the blankets and how it felt when he'd grabbed my breast in his sleep.

What should I do?

I continued to sit in the dark, staring at Konner and feeling miserable.

"Runa," he mouthed in his sleep.

My heart leapt as my stomach dropped. *I have to protect him. That's my most important duty. He'll never know what I saw in his dreams. He will awaken and obtain his magic as planned.*

Konner awoke in a panic, frantic that his dreams had given him away.

"Did you sleep well?" I asked, glancing over my shoulder as I stood at the window.

"Um, yes. You?" He was still suspicious.

"I didn't get much sleep."

He breathed a sigh of relief. *If I didn't sleep, I couldn't share his dreams.*

"I'm sorry to hear that," he responded half-heartedly.

"Well, I'm going and get dressed. Meet you downstairs?"

He nodded.

I returned to my room and congratulated myself on my performance. Konner didn't suspect that I'd seen anything.

17

In the days that followed, Rowan seemed determined to prove to me he would be a good mate. The effort on his part was unnecessary because he was right. He didn't have to point out that we got along well or that we were a good team. I really wanted to fall for Rowan. A romance with him would be so easy and straightforward. But Konner was my top priority. He had to be.

Still, Rowan heeded my request that our relationship be platonic for the time being. I'd realized Rowan's first impression of Konner's jealousy had been correct, but I still had to keep our interactions nonsexual to maintain the ruse that I didn't know Konner's desires.

Konner was upset and distracted by Rowan's behavior. Every time he twinged with resentment, I renewed my promise to pretend nothing had happened.

Of course, Wilhelm helped on that front. Every

few hours, he received a sealed letter on the messages table. He always grabbed it before Ed and Kat noticed and took it to the library to read. Then he wrote a response and gave it to Konner.

After the third time I'd seen this exchange, I followed Konner to the messages table where he took the response. When he placed the envelope on the transportation circle carved into the top of the table, I asked, "Do you want me to ask one of your parents to send that for you?"

"No need." He grinned at me. "I have enough magic for this."

He whispered the spell. A yellow light flashed, and the paper was gone.

"Wow. Great job, Konner," I praised.

He flushed, pleased.

"But what is all this about?"

Konner pulled me into the library before explaining. "Midsummer is in a few days."

My heart pounded in response. *Not that time again.* The fae night of mischief was dreaded by guardians across Faerie.

"Don't tell me you and Wilhelm are planning to participate."

They grinned and nodded, looking like the brothers they were.

"Absolutely not," I protested. "How could you even think about it? You live in a border town. It's way too dangerous." *Sure, Mikhail and his friends always celebrated Midsummer, but we had extra guards for protection.*

"Aw, come on, Runa," Wilhelm whined. "I've never gotten to celebrate before and neither has Konner. Rowan couldn't protect us both. Plus, this is Konner's last chance since he's awakening in a few months."

I turned my glare toward Rowan, whose eyes widened. "You're okay with this?"

He shrugged. "It should be fine for one night. Even in times of war, people need to have some fun."

I thought about telling Kat and Ed, but I knew it wouldn't do any good. Fae parents all knew about Midsummer. It was practically a tradition for them to ignore their children running wild and taking risks for one night a year. I sighed heavily, and Rowan wrapped an arm around my shoulders.

"We aren't going to be alone, either. We'll have at least another three guardians helping us," he reassured.

Konner pursed his lips at Rowan touching me. I put some distance between us and stepped toward Konner.

"Is this something you really want?" I asked him.

He looked at his little brother. Wilhelm's round eyes pleaded as he clasped his hands together. Konner nodded at me. "Yeah, it's my last chance to celebrate Midsummer with Wilhelm."

I gnawed on my lower lip. "Fine."

Wilhelm cheered and threw his arms wide to hug me. Konner stepped between us, and Rowan dragged Wilhelm back to the table.

The next few days were filled with secret preparations. When the morning of the summer solstice dawned, Wilhelm could barely contain his excitement.

Even Kat had a difficult time keeping the smile

off her face as she tried to ignore what was going on. She busied herself making honey buns, which none of us were allowed to eat.

As dusk approached, we all went about our business as usual. Rowan and I even checked the perimeter like always.

When the time for bed came, Wilhelm made a big show of yawning and calling it a night. Ed smiled into his tea, and Kat snickered quietly.

We all went to our respective rooms. Rowan and I shifted to wolf form as Konner and Wilhelm donned dark clothes for the night ahead. Then we each snuck downstairs in the quiet house.

We crept out of the front door and closed it gently behind us. A basket of honey buns, covered with a checkered cloth, sat on the porch near the steps.

I had no idea what prank Konner and Wilhelm had planned with their friends. I was much more concerned with keeping them safe. Rowan and I kept careful watch while they retrieved a sack from the barn.

"All right, let's go," Wilhelm whispered.

I was on high alert, my ear twitching at every sound as we took the road away from town. Halfway to the nearest farm, I heard the scuffing of shoes on dirt before I saw three faelings and their guardians appear from out of the darkness.

"So glad you could join us this year," the oldest of the three faelings said when we'd reached them.

"I'm so ready!" Wilhelm cheered.

Rowan and I nodded to the other wolves before we moved to form a loose circle around the faelings.

As we started walking toward their first target,

the only female faeling turned to Konner. "We heard your intended bondmate finally showed up."

I heard Konner sigh internally, but he nodded to her. "This is Runa," he said, gesturing toward me. "Runa, this is Willa, her brothers, Charlie and Wes, and their bondmates, Keita, Lars, and Anyte."

I spared a glance for each of them.

As we approached the farmhouse, everyone hushed. We snuck up to the porch and found a basket of cookies. The faelings seemed almost disappointed at the bribe. They each took a cookie and moved on.

The second stop had not made an offering to mischievous fae on the prowl.

Grinning at each other, the faelings searched the fields for a scarecrow.

Being the tallest, Konner took it off its post. Charlie removed its head with a knife from his pocket. Wilhelm could barely muffle his laughter as he reached into his sack and pulled out a donkey head made of cloth. Wes and Willa replaced the scarecrow's head with the donkey's, and Konner put it back on its post.

Once they'd gotten farther away, they all howled with laughter. My heart warmed to see Konner having so much fun.

I guess it's a little funny to think about how the farmer will react tomorrow.

The night was quiet while they sought their next straw-filled victim. A glint of light caught my eye as the clouds parted overhead to reveal the rare full solstice moon. Its glorious orange hue made me sniff deeply in astonishment.

And then I froze. A gentle breeze carried the last

scent I ever wanted to smell. My heart hammered painfully in my chest.

Vampires.

"Stop!" I told Konner through the bond. *"We've got trouble."*

His fear pumped in my veins, and he halted the other fae with a gesture.

Every wolf moved to guard his or her faeling as we tightened out protective circle, our hackles raised at the unseen threat.

I sniffed the air deeply, filling my nose with the sickening scent. *How close? How many?*

My ears strained for any sound, but they arrived as silently as a nightmare, beckoned by our dread.

They're skin was as horrifying as I remembered, ashen and unnatural. Their eyes glowed, reflecting the moon's light and mocking the beauty I'd just admired. Their lips sneered at us, revealing canines as sharp and as deadly as my own.

"Don't worry, Konner." I tried to calm him as his fear closed my throat. *"I will protect you."*

There were twice as many vampires as there were wolves, but I refused to lose anyone else.

I knew we had to move fast before they surrounded us. As soon as the one nearest me twitched, I launched into my attack, and the rest of the wolves followed. I latched onto the fiend's arm as it raised its hand to defend itself, and Rowan took it down by the throat with a snarl.

Seeking another target in the fray of fur and fangs, my stomach dropped as one vampire closed in on Konner from behind. As it wrapped its arms around him, Konner stomped on its foot and elbowed it in the stomach before spinning around to kick it in the head.

It went down with eyes wide, and Anyte was there to finish it off.

When its shriek had faded into silence, I took that moment to throw my head back and howl, warning anyone within earshot that vampires were near.

My howl turned into a yelp when a vampire cuffed me on the snout. I blinked past the tears just as it stood over me. Its long fingers reached for my throat, ready to tear me apart. A vicious growl sounded a second before Rowan jumped it from behind.

I shook my head and got to my feet. I'd thought we were fending them off, but as I took in the battle, I saw we were still outnumbered.

Wes and Willa clung to each other, whimpering while Charlie wrapped his arms protectively around them. Their guardians were surrounded, and the vampires were slowly closing in.

Snarling and snapping at a vampire who was reaching for Konner, I didn't see the one that grabbed Wilhelm, but I heard him cry out.

I watched in horror as Isla's gruesome death was about to repeat itself right before my eyes. As it brought its fangs to his throat, a pack of reinforcements burst onto the scene. Ten unknown werewolves announced their arrivals with snarls and growls.

The vampire that held Wilhelm dropped him to defend itself from two charging wolves.

"Grab Wilhelm, and let's get out of here," I barked at Konner through the bond.

After dragging his brother to his feet, they started to run toward home with Rowan and I close behind and the other faelings and their bondmates after. As we passed through the clash, I thought I smelled something familiar.

Pushing it aside for a less life-threatening moment, I glanced behind me to ensure we weren't being pursued.

If any vampires tried to follow us, they didn't make it past the wolves who'd come to the rescue. When we burst through the front door, Ed and Kat were waiting at the entrance. Wilhelm ran to his mother's arms as they both wept in relief.

Konner embraced his father. "Thank the gods you're all safe," Ed whispered.

I trembled as the tension in my muscles relaxed. Rowan leaned up against me, providing what comfort he could. But even as I started to breathe easy, my limbs numbed with Konner's shock.

"I'm here, Konner. You're home. Everyone is safe."

He breathed deep and let it out slowly a few times before my heart started to calm with his.

After a while, Kat turned puffy, red eyes in our direction. "Thank you for keeping my boys safe."

I was exhausted as I climbed the stairs, but I shifted to human form long enough to wash the stench of vampire blood off me. I stared at my own reflection in the bathroom mirror. *Her wide eyes and pale cheeks couldn't be me. You didn't lose anyone else tonight. Everyone is safe,* I told her.

When I'd scratched at Konner's bedroom door, he didn't even question why I was there. In light of what I'd learned from his dreams, I knew I should've put some space between us. But I needed to be near him, and I knew he needed me as well. I curled on top of his blankets beside him. With every stroke of his fingers in my fur, he calmed a little. And with every steady beat of his heart, he told me he was safe.

18

When I went downstairs the next morning, Ed, Kat, Wilhelm, and Rowan were standing near the messages table. There was an opened envelope in the transportation circle. Ed read whatever it had contained over Kat's shoulder. Rowan and Wilhelm stood by for news.

"What does it say?" Konner asked, coming down the stairs behind me.

Kat looked up from the paper. "Every faeling is to evacuate until further notice."

"Where do we have to go?" Konner asked, businesslike.

"There's a place for people who have nowhere else to go, but it suggests staying with family or friends. I think I should send a message to Naiha and Byron. With them both being in large cities, there are hardly ever vampire attacks. But neither of them really have room for all of you for an extended period, so you should probably split up."

"I'll go to Uncle Byron's," Wilhelm volunteered.

Konner nodded his agreement, and Kat went to the library to write the letters.

"You all had better pack a bag so you're ready," Ed instructed us.

We went upstairs to comply. As I packed, a knock sounded on my hall door. It was Rowan.

"Do you need any help?" he asked for something to say.

"No, thanks. I got it."

He stepped close to me and took my hand, and I didn't stop him.

"You really had my back out there. Thank you," I whispered.

"I told you we make a good team." He smiled gently. "Please be careful, Runa. I know you can handle yourself, but stay safe. Okay?"

I nodded. "You too."

Packed and ready, we went downstairs, and I took a seat beside Konner. Konner eyed Rowan suspiciously as he followed me.

"He just wanted to tell me to keep us safe," I explained.

His tension eased a little, and I cursed internally at his reaction.

We ate a hurried breakfast while we waited for Naiha's and Byron's positive replies, which came shortly.

"How long do you think we will be gone?" Wilhelm asked as we readied to leave.

"It's hard to say. Anywhere from a couple weeks to a few months," Kat replied.

"Are you all ready?" Ed asked.

We nodded.

We walked to the depot together. There were no signs of vampires on the way there. The depot was crowded with faelings and their bondmates evacuating to safer locations, and I was relieved to see Charlie and his siblings safe with their guardians.

"Your Aunt Naiha promised to send someone to the depot on her end in case you don't remember the way," Kat told Konner.

Konner nodded his understanding.

We grabbed our bags and prepared to leave. We both hugged everyone and promised to stay safe. At the conductor's signal, Konner and I stepped into the transportation circle. We waved goodbye, and the yellow light flashed.

The depot we stood in was much bigger than the one we'd left. There were multiple transportation circles, and many fae bustled about their business.

I instinctively reached for Konner's hand so we wouldn't be separated in the crowd. I bit my lip when I'd felt his arousal flush my cheeks. I squashed my answering lust before my response could reach him. *I need to be more careful not to provoke his desire.*

We walked past the transportation circles to the atrium. Konner looked around, then waved his free arm at a fae a little older than us. She ran toward us and launched herself at Konner. He dropped my hand to catch her in a bear hug.

"Konner, you've gotten tall!" she gushed, astonished.

He smiled at her. "And I think you shrank," he teased.

"Shut up!" She punched him in the arm but laughed.

"Runa, this is my cousin, Keyri. Keyri, my bondmate, Runa," Konner introduced.

"Runa? *The* Runa?" Keyri asked.

Konner nodded.

"You don't say! Well, better late than never, eh Runa?"

"Keyri—" Konner censured.

"It's fine, Konner. She's right. I'm glad to finally be with Konner, and it's nice to meet you, Keyri."

"Glad to hear it. You too."

We shook hands. Then we followed her toward the exit.

"Where's Aunt Naiha?" Konner asked.

"Taking the world by storm, of course."

"Naturally," Konner responded, then turned to me. "Keyri's mother, my Aunt Naiha, is a merchant. She handles all the sales and marketing for our farm and others. She's my mom's older sister. That's actually how my parents met: through my aunt."

"Yeah, she's great at hooking everyone up but herself," Keyri added.

"My uncle left Aunt Naiha when Keyri was very young. She has never remated."

"She doesn't have time," Keyri quoted.

"What about you? You awakened a year ago."

"I'm not even thinking about that right now. I have way too much to do and see before I start a family."

"Yeah? You're lucky." Konner winced.

"Aunt Kat is pushing hard, huh?"

He nodded.

"Well, buck up, Cuz. I can get you into all kinds

of trouble before you go home. We may even find you a completely inappropriate mate that your parents will hate. Maybe they'll give up."

Konner wallowed in the face of Keyri's laughter.

I reached out to comfort him and froze. *My comfort in this situation will only make things worse. But if I don't comfort him, I will be acting strange. Will he figure out that I know?*

Keyri jumped on his back for a piggyback ride. "Hey, one day at a time. All right?"

He nodded.

She messed up his hair. "All right?"

"Yes!"

She grinned and jumped down. "Good. Then follow me to adventure!"

It was difficult not to be affected by Keyri's infectious good mood. Konner and I were both enjoying ourselves as we left the crowded depot and stepped into the street.

"To the left, you will see the harbor of our beautiful city, Imani, and to the right, the city. Any questions?"

"Just one: you aren't planning on quitting your day job to become a tour guide, are you?" Konner teased.

"There goes my life's one aspiration."

They laughed.

It was enlightening to see this side of Konner. He was so playful with Keyri. I smiled to see him relaxed and having fun. *It was a good decision to send him here.*

We walked near the harbor, passing docks with huge merchant ships and busy warehouses, where fae loaded crates for shipping. Finally, we entered a residential area with tall houses that were smooshed together.

"Here we are." Keyri pointed to one of the identical smooshed homes.

We walked up the stairs, and she unlocked the door, motioning us to go ahead of her.

19

We entered a sitting room and took the stairs to the second floor. To the left was a kitchen and dining room, and to the right was another sitting room. We continued up the stairs to the third floor. We passed a couple of closed doors. At the end of the hall, Keyri opened a door.

"This is where you'll be staying," she said.

The room had two beds separated by a small table. Across from the beds was a dresser with a large mirror on top.

I could feel Konner's embarrassed pleasure at getting to sleep in the same room, and I ignored it.

"Well, I'll let you get settled. Mom will be back at dinnertime. I'll make lunch in a little while. Come down if you're hungry." Keyri shut the door as she left.

"Which side do you prefer?" I asked like this was normal.

"Whichever." Konner shrugged his shoulders while a slight blush dusted his cheeks.

I took the window side and started to put my clothes in the dresser as the tension built.

"Your cousin seems nice."

"Yeah, she's great. I always have fun when she's around."

The silence was thick as I searched for something else to say.

"Can you show me where the bathroom is?"

He nodded and showed me to a door next to ours in the hallway. Shutting the door behind me, I splashed cold water on my face and took a deep breath.

I decided to pretend like nothing happened. It doesn't matter if the setting has changed or that we're sharing a room until further notice.

I stared at my reflection in the bathroom mirror. A drop of water dripped off the end of my nose, and I felt Konner's arousal from his memory.

Get a grip, Runa. You hear me? What's the most important? Getting Konner through his awakening. Act normal. That means don't be afraid to show affection toward him, either, just like before. Be natural. He's your bondmate and your friend. Don't overthink it. It's just Konner.

I dried my face and took a deep breath.

When I entered our bedroom, Konner sat at the edge of his bed.

"Hey," I smiled at him. "So it looks like we could be here for a while. What do you want to do?"

"I'm not sure. Let's talk to my aunt tonight and see if she needs any help. There's a giant bookstore nearby. Do you want to go after lunch?"

"Sounds great. But before lunch, I think we

should send a message to your parents telling them we arrived safely."

"Good idea."

We went to the study on the first floor. Konner wrote a quick note and transported it home.

Keyri made a simple but tasty lunch. We told her about our plans to go to the bookstore after we ate.

"I might've guessed you'd go there first," she teased Konner. "I actually need to go there, too. I have to get a book for my ancient Elvish class."

"Are you taking classes? Doesn't Aunt Naiha want you to take over for her?"

"Of course, she wants to keep the business in the family, but she doesn't want to force me. I haven't really decided what I want to do yet, so I'm taking some required classes and some that interest me."

Warmth flooded my chest as Konner filled with longing.

"If your aunt is so understanding, maybe your parents will be, too," I suggested through the bond.

"My aunt is different. My parents are far more traditional."

I didn't push him any more.

After we had eaten, we all walked to the bookstore. Konner hadn't been exaggerating. The place was huge. It took up a whole city block.

I looked around with pure excitement, then turned to Konner. He smiled at my joy, pleased he'd made me happy.

Keyri told us to meet her at the front when we were finished and went off to find her book.

I wasn't about to separate from Konner, so we went to the human studies section first. As he browsed earnestly, I skimmed the titles absent-mindedly.

One shelf over, a skinny, recently-awakened fae stood on a ladder trying to reach a book. I could see he was going to fall by the way his tiptoes teetered on the step.

"Whoa!" I steadied his hips, holding him up as he started to fall.

He gripped the ladder and slowly climbed down. His face was beet red when he turned toward me.

"Th-thank you," he stammered shyly.

"No problem," I responded.

He was a couple inches shorter than I was.

"Which book were you after? I can get it for you," I offered.

He thanked me again and told me the title, pointing to the top shelf.

"Do you mind holding the ladder for me?" I asked.

As I climbed, he gripped the ladder so it wouldn't roll away.

"What happened? Are you all right?" I heard Konner ask the fae from below.

"I'm fine. Thank you," he said, even more embarrassed.

After retrieving the book, I climbed down the ladder and turned around. Konner held the sides of the ladder, encircling me. My heart thumped and I gasped, surprised that his face was so close to mine.

"Konner, you surprised me." I laughed nervously.

Strangely, his face was impassive, and the bond gave me no indication of how he was feeling.

Is he blocking me?

My only clue to his emotions was that his fists clenched the ladder behind me.

"Thanks for holding the ladder for me." I reached up and gently placed my fingertips on his inner elbow.

He dropped his arm and let me out.

I handed the book to the skinny fae. "Is this right?"

He took it and smiled self-consciously. "Yes, thank you." His eyes shifted from me to over my shoulder where Konner stood. His smile faltered, and he hurried away.

I sighed inwardly. *Fae...*

"Did you find anything good?" I asked Konner.

He held his treasure out to me.

"Greek history and mythology, huh? The Greeks are Europeans, right?"

He nodded enthusiastically, and joy sparkled in his eyes.

I wasn't in the mood for heavy reading at the moment. I picked a romance novel about two young wolves from rival packs who fell in love. It was sure to be predictable and emotionally satisfying.

"I didn't know you like romance, Runa," Konner said as we waited for Keyri.

"Sure, I do. Our mating rituals may be designed for rational choice, but some wolves are lucky enough to mate for love. Isn't it the same for fae?"

He looked at his feet as my heart sank with his dejection. "Yeah, some are lucky enough."

Stupid, Runa. You idiot.

20

*K*onner's aunt arrived just as Keyri was putting dinner on the table.

"Sorry I'm late. Thank you for making dinner, Keyri. Konner, I can't believe how tall you've gotten." She hugged Konner tightly. "And this must be Runa."

"Thank you for having us," I said.

"Anytime. We're relaxed here, so make yourself at home."

I nodded.

As we ate, Konner turned to his aunt, his face an expressionless mask. "What would you like me to do while I'm here, Aunt Naiha? Do you need help with anything?"

She raised her eyebrows and put down her fork. "I'd love your help, Konner, but only if it's what *you* want. You could come to work with me and learn our side of the business, you could go with Keyri and hang out at the university, or you could choose something else that interests you. I know plenty of tradesmen if you're interested in that."

Keyri looked at him as if saying, "I told you so."

Konner's gratitude filled the bond. He glanced at me for guidance.

"Whatever you want, I'll be there with you."

"I think I'd enjoy going to see the university with Keyri."

Naiha nodded and started to eat again.

"This will be fun," Keyri said. "You won't be able to take classes since you aren't awakened yet, but you can go to the library. Plus, there's always something happening on campus."

Konner's eyes were bright, and he didn't even attempt to keep the smile off his face. The little flame of hope he felt for the future flickered through the bond. Its warmth melted my heart a little.

After dinner, we had tea in the second-floor sitting room. At Naiha's request, Konner updated her on how everyone was at home. She was pleased Kat was happy, and Wilhelm seemed to be growing up nicely.

Afterward, Naiha excused herself and went to her room to work. Keyri went to the study to do homework, and Konner and I read our new books in the second-floor sitting room.

While getting ready for bed, I realized I didn't own any pajama bottoms. Keyri let me borrow a pair until I could purchase some. I changed in the bathroom while Konner changed in the bedroom. Before entering, I knocked softly at the door.

"Come in," Konner called.

As he climbed into bed, I saw he wore a snug-fit, short-sleeved shirt and pajama pants.

I crossed the room and got into my bed.

Konner lay on his side, facing me. "Goodnight, Runa," he whispered.

"'Night," I replied and blew out the lamp.

I could see him clearly in the dark, staring blindly in my direction. I watched him for a while. Finally, I asked, *"Can't you sleep?"*

"I'm wondering how different my life could be."

"You can reach for whatever you want, but there's always a price when you take risks. It takes a lot of courage to face potential loss."

"I guess I'm not very brave."

"It's not always the smartest decision to take risks, and you have a strong sense of duty."

"At the cost of my own happiness."

"Everything has a price."

"Is the price too high?"

"That's for you to decide, Konner. But know: I'm with you whatever you choose."

His longing shot through the bond again.

I want to give him everything he wishes for, whatever it takes to return the smile to his face. But I can't choose for him. He has to decide his own path. I can only try to protect him on whatever path he chooses until his awakening, and then I have to let him go.

Sadness overwhelmed me. I tried to keep it to myself, but Konner soon felt it. He got out of his bed and felt his way in the dark to mine. He sat on the edge. *"What's wrong, Runa? Did I upset you?"*

"No, Konner. It's not you. I was thinking how empty a promise with an expiration date is."

Our yearning and sorrow mixed into a depressing pity parade. We trudged down a path chosen for us, too closed-in to deviate. Exhausted by the myriad of emotions, Konner's proximity was comforting. I don't know when I fell asleep.

I awoke when I felt hair tickling my cheek. I opened my eyes to find it was Konner's hair. He lay, sleeping and facing me in the same small bed. I sat up quickly and nearly fell off my bed.

Okay. This seriously needs to stop. I looked down at Konner, ready to tell him just that. But, as the morning sun filtered through the curtains and shone off his hidden copper strands, I couldn't make myself do it. Instead, I did something I knew I shouldn't. I reached out and gently stroked the shining threads. They were soft and glossy like silk.

When he hadn't noticed, I got brave. I moved the hair from his face and stared at him, etching every line and curve in my mind. Then I ran the back of my finger near his eyelid, letting his thick, dark lashes tickle my skin. *That's enough, Runa.* I censured myself harshly and left him in my bed.

After collecting my clothes and bath products, I went to the bathroom. I knew when Konner awoke by the feeling of disappointment and loss that flooded the bond. I sank deeper into the bath, trying to drown out my conflicting emotions. *Remember your mission.*

Attempting to avoid further complications, I braided my long hair—as I reconsidered cutting it— and splashed my face with cold water to reduce my warm-bath complexion.

There was no response when I had knocked on the bedroom door. *Konner must be downstairs.* I entered the bedroom to put my things away.

Konner was pulling a shirt on over his head.

I couldn't help but notice the smooth skin

stretched tight across his abdomen and the V of his pelvis above his pants. I got just a glimpse, but it was enough to whet my palate.

Though I tried to control my facial expression, Konner was still embarrassed when he saw I was there.

"Good morning," I greeted normally. "Sorry to barge in. I knocked."

"I didn't hear."

"So what's on the schedule for today? Keyri won't have school until tomorrow."

"I don't know. Let's go down to breakfast and ask her what she's doing."

Konner helped Keyri prepare breakfast, and I stayed out of their way.

"Do you have plans today?" Konner asked her.

"Well, I need to go to the market, but ancient Elvish is kicking my ass. I really have to translate my homework for tomorrow. Would you mind going to the market for me? I'll give you a list and the money you need."

"No problem. Right, Runa?"

I nodded.

"Thanks. That will be a big help."

I washed the dishes as Konner bathed and Keyri studied. The only thing I could think about was my warm, soapy hands on Konner's stomach. I censured myself harshly again to little avail. My only victory was keeping my thoughts and feelings to myself.

"Need help?" Konner asked, suddenly beside me.

I dropped the plate I was rinsing, and it crashed to the floor.

"Damn it. I'm sorry. I'll clean it up." I rushed to pick up the shattered plate.

Konner knelt to help.

"Don't worry about it, Konner. It's my mess, and I don't want you to cut—ow." I sliced my finger on the sharp glass. Blood welled and slowly drip off my finger.

"Are you all right?" Konner worried, grabbing my hand to see how deep the cut was. "It doesn't look too bad," he reassured, examining my finger closely.

Before I could stop him, he brought my finger into his mouth and sucked on it gently.

My entire body flushed, and I stared at him, astonished. His lips were soft, and his tongue was warm and wet as it caressed my finger. My cut stung sweetly as he licked it. I shivered.

It felt like forever before I got ahold of myself, but it was probably only a few seconds. "Konner…" I gently pulled my hand away. I met his eyes seriously, and he didn't look away.

"I'll get a broom and a bandage," he whispered after a while.

I went to the sink and washed my cut, trying to forget the feel of Konner's mouth on me. By the time he returned, I'd suppressed the encounter.

He wrapped my cut and cleaned up my mess, looking a little too smug.

What are you doing, Konner?

21

rmed with a list and cloth bags for purchases, Konner and I set out toward the market. Seagulls called over the sound of ship bells as they glided on the refreshing breeze. I closed my eyes and breathed deep, enjoying the summer air. Not far from the harbor, permanent and temporary stalls had been set up. Farmers, butchers, and bakers were all there to sell their food.

Because Konner knew more about cooking, I let him lead the way and pick the best products. He was in a good mood as we moved through the crowded market and haggled with vendors.

When we'd purchased everything on the list, we sat on a quiet dock and ate fresh cinnamon rolls. Konner cheerfully chewed his reward and gazed out over the water.

"You're in a good mood." I pointed out.

"I am. I have everything I want. I'm going to the university tomorrow, and, right now, it's just you and me."

"It is nice here, but I like it at home, too," I countered.

"It's too crowded and stuffy at home."

When we had returned, Konner made lunch. Keyri was grateful, ate quickly, and returned to studying.

Because it was such a nice day and the breeze from the harbor was so fresh, Konner and I sat on the front steps for the rest of the afternoon, watching the water and the seagulls and reading in the sunshine.

That night, I didn't wait for Konner to fall asleep, nor did I encourage him in any way to come to me. I wished him goodnight, blew out the lamp, and turned my back to him. I could feel his disappointment, but I knew it was better that way.

Konner was up early the next morning, excited about his first visit to a university. When everyone was ready, we went to the depot to catch a regularly scheduled transport farther into the city. We crammed into the transportation circle with a bunch of strangers. The depot we arrived in was equally crowded, but mostly consisted of recently awakened fae.

We followed Keyri out of the depot and onto campus. The university's campus was bustling with students, who hurried between the many buildings. Most of the students were fae, but every now and then, I spotted a werewolf.

Keyri stopped in front of a brick building with large glass windows. "This is the Human Studies Department. That's where you were headed, right? I'll stop by after class to pick you up." She waved at us and hurried to her class.

Konner looked at me excitedly. I smiled and nodded, encouraging him to go ahead. He opened the glass door, and we went inside. The atrium was large, and the strangest noise echoed off the walls. It sounded like music, but it was unlike any music I'd ever heard.

"What is that?" I asked.

"I don't know. Let's find out."

We followed the sound down a hallway and into an open sitting room. The chairs and tables had been pushed to the walls, and two fae were dancing wildly in the center of the room. They hopped and twirled. The man even lifted the woman into the air a few times. Another couple watched them carefully as if trying to memorize the steps. A fifth fae stood near the source of the sound. It was a box with a horn attached and a spinning disk on top. Upon closer inspection, I saw the fae near the music maker was the one I'd helped at the bookstore. When the song had ended, the skinny fae stopped the spinning disk.

The watching couple clapped enthusiastically, and Konner and I joined in, drawing everyone's attention. Recognition formed in the skinny fae's eyes, and I waved at him.

"Hello again," I said, and everyone turned to him.

"Do you know them, Ryuu?" the dancing female fae asked him.

"We met at the bookstore the other day," Ryuu explained.

"My cousin goes here, and I've always been interested in human studies. So we thought we'd stop by," Konner explained.

"Ah, well then, welcome," the dancing male greeted. "I'm Salem, and this is Riku," he introduced, indicating his dancing partner. "You already met Ryuu. This is Ezio and Raven. And you are?"

"I'm Konner, and this is my bondmate, Runa."

"Welcome, Konner and Runa. Let us know if you have any questions," Riku encouraged, smiling.

Konner thanked her and pointed to the box with the horn. "What's that?"

"A phonograph," Ryuu answered. "Humans record music on these disks, called records, and use a record player to listen to the recorded music. Their technology has far surpassed the phonograph, and records for that matter. But, because we don't have electricity in Faerie, this is all we can use here."

Konner analyzed the phonograph closely.

"Human music? Does it all sound like that?" I asked.

"Not at all," Raven answered. "They have many different genres of music. We were just listening to swing because Salem and Riku were teaching us how to dance to it. Swing isn't listened to much in the human realm anymore except by the older generation, which makes it easy for us to find records."

Konner looked up from Ryuu showing him how the phonograph worked. "Do you mind if we try, too?" he asked excitedly.

They smiled their consent.

Salem and Riku showed us, as well as Raven and Ezio, how to stand. We all learned the basic steps. I'd seen fae dancing at many of the parties Mikhail went to. It was characterized by complicated formalized steps and not much contact between partners. Swing dancing was a lot more like werewolf dancing. It was driven by the beat with only a few set steps and many embellishments.

"Swing is all about the beat and improvisations. Trust your partner and follow him," Salem instructed.

Konner was good at leading, and we were soon confident in the basics.

"You guys catch on fast," Salem praised. "Hey, are you up for a real challenge?" He smiled mischievously.

We nodded, ready for whatever he had.

"Ryuu, play 'Sing, Sing, Sing.'" Salem grinned.

Riku and Salem stood ready with the rest of us.

As my hands rested in Konner's, I looked up into his eyes. They sparkled with joy, and I couldn't help but smile back.

I want him to stay this happy forever.

The song started with a drumbeat and was soon accompanied by an upbeat assortment of blaring instruments. The tempo was fast, but Konner was ready.

We kept it simple, adding only a few spins. Konner led, and I followed. Though our steps weren't as advanced as Salem's and Riku's, it was still fun. By the time the song was over, my heart pumped hard from exertion. Everyone smiled and laughed.

"Whoa, look at the time!" Ezio exclaimed. "We're going to be late for class. See you around," he called as he, Raven, and Salem ran from the room.

Ryuu played a softer song, and we all helped

Riku move the chairs and tables back to their normal positions. After which, we all sat.

"Are you going to major in human studies once you awaken, Konner?" Riku asked conversationally.

"I want to, but my parents want me to stay and help on the farm."

"I can see this is a difficult topic. I'm sorry," she apologized.

"It's fine. What's your emphasis in human studies?"

"I'm interested in human medicine. My brother, Ryuu, studies human technology. What interests you the most?"

I looked more closely at Riku and Ryuu. They did look like siblings. They had the same petite builds and the same blue eyes. But while Ryuu had golden brown hair, Riku had strawberry blonde.

"Everything. It all fascinates me. It would be difficult to choose an emphasis."

They both bobbed their heads in understanding.

"What about you, Runa? What will you do once Konner awakens?" Riku asked.

"I'm not really sure yet. I'll probably choose a mate and eventually ask my alpha to find me a job."

Konner listened intently. He'd never heard my future plans, or lack thereof.

"It's important to keep the pup population up," Riku approved. "Do you have any promising mate candidates?"

I really didn't want to answer in front of Konner, but that would've been rude and suspicious. I nodded and answered truthfully. "Two." *This is better for Konner anyway. The sooner he lets go of this foolish desire, the better off he'll be.*

Konner's expression was cold and uninterested, and I got nothing from the bond.

"How long are you in town?" Ryuu asked.

"We aren't sure," I answered.

"Well, feel free to come here when you have free time. There's almost always someone in the lounge. We have a great selection of records you can listen to. Raven is studying human music, and I'm sure she wouldn't mind answering any questions you have. Also, you're more than welcome to join us when we go on outings."

"Thank you. I'm sure we'll be here often." I looked at Konner for a response.

He nodded silently.

22

After chatting a while longer, Riku and Ryuu had to go to class. Konner and I went outside to eat our packed lunches in a big grassy area. Then we walked around, checking out the campus.

As we strolled back to the Human Studies Department, we saw Keyri holding hands with a fae student. She didn't see us, but we were both surprised when she kissed him before saying goodbye.

We met Keyri outside the Human Studies Department. As we walked to the depot, Konner broached the subject. "I thought you weren't even thinking of mating right now, Keyri?"

"I'm not."

"Oh? Then who was that you were kissing?" he teased.

"That's my boyfriend, Shayne."

Konner was astounded.

"Don't you think it's better to try someone out

rather than jump into being mated to him or her for the rest of your life?"

"I guess…"

"If things like this were more common, maybe my dad wouldn't have left."

Konner was silent, not knowing how to respond.

"What are they doing to you out there in the country? A lot is changing, Konner. There are many options for recently-awakened fae. You don't just have to do what Aunt Kat and Uncle Ed want you to do. You can choose for yourself."

I was surprised by Keyri's sentiment. It was unusual to hear fae talk about going against their elders. *Of course, Naiha seems to give Keyri a lot of freedom to make her own choices.*

Konner's eyes grew distant like he had a lot to think about. He remained deep in thought, pondering the possibilities, for the rest of the evening.

As we lay in the dark that night, he asked, *"Do you really think anything is possible for me, Runa?"*

"For you? I think you put a lot of pressure on yourself, and I believe your parents are more understanding than you think they are. I agree with Keyri. You have a lot of options. Not everyone is so lucky."

"But what about you? You can do whatever you want once I awaken."

"Well, not whatever I want. My alpha certainly has a say, but you're right. I don't have parents to impose their expectations on me. That also means I'll be alone except for my pack." I wasn't upset he'd brought it up. I'd long come to terms with loneliness.

"You won't be alone. You have two mate candidates."

Yeah, but I don't love them, I said to myself. As I fell

asleep, I tried not to think about why that suddenly bothered me.

For the next couple weeks, Konner and I went to the university with Keyri. We spent a lot of time listening to records. Raven was quite knowledgeable about human music. Konner talked to her at great length about instruments and the shift in popular genres over time. After a while, Konner had discovered rock 'n' roll.

Salem was studying human history, and Ezio studied human literature. I enjoyed talking to Ezio about the human books he'd read. I tried to get him to recommend just one title he thought represented all of human literature. He said it was impossible to choose only one. "Humans have been writing for too long and in too many languages to choose only one," he'd told me. However, he promised to bring me back a book the next time they went to the human realm.

Konner and I had fun while around the human studies majors, Konner in particular. He fit in so well with them that I hoped he would decide to tell his parents what he really wanted. On the other hand, studying humans in books was significantly less dangerous than interacting with them in person. The thought of Konner going to the human realm made me nervous, and I scolded myself. *He'll have his full magic once he awakens and will be more than capable of protecting himself. Besides, it's not my place to worry about what he does after he awakens.* The unease I felt didn't go away even though I was confident in Konner's abilities. No matter how worried I was, I never let Konner know. I heartily encouraged him to find his happiness.

One day, we all sat in the lounge listening to a band with the same name as an insect.

"Let's do something this weekend," Salem suggested while flipping through a human publication, which was mostly pictures on thin, shiny paper.

"Like what?" Riku asked.

Salem shrugged and continued to stare at the pages absently.

"We could go to the human realm and see a movie," Ezio suggested. Alarm shot through me.

"But then Runa and Konner can't come," Riku pointed out. I exhaled, relieved.

"What about this?" Salem said, holding up a photo of two practically naked humans at the beach.

"A beach party?" Raven asked.

"A human beach party," Salem clarified.

"What's the difference?" I asked.

"We wear human bathing clothes," Riku explained.

"But we don't have anything like that," Konner said.

"I'm sure we have spares lying around somewhere," Riku responded.

"So tomorrow at Pike Beach?" Salem suggested.

"Everyone bring some food for lunch. We can have a cookout," Raven added.

"I'll find swimwear for Konner and Runa," Riku promised.

We all agreed, excited about our outing.

The following day was warm and sunny, the perfect day to go to the beach. Konner packed strawberries and peaches for dessert. Pike Beach wasn't far from Naiha's, so we walked.

Konner had a spring in his step. He smiled without care, and the copper in his hair shone in the midmorning sun.

I was blissfully content with his mood and life in general. On a day such as that, everything was colored with cheer. It felt like it would always be as perfect as it was at that moment.

When we'd reached the cream-colored sand of Pike Beach, we removed our shoes and let the warm powder caress our bare feet.

Riku and Ryuu waved at us from down the beach. Riku wore swim clothes that barely covered her. There were two pieces. The bottom looked like underwear, and the top a very short undershirt that just covered her breasts. Ryuu wore short pants that ended just before his knees and no shirt.

Konner analyzed the clothes, or lack thereof, with fascination. When we'd reached them, Riku handed Konner a pair of short pants like Ryuu's and beckoned for me to follow her to the beach's bathroom.

Konner followed and stood close by while I went in to change.

"Is this really what humans wear to the beach?" I asked Riku as she handed me the swim clothes she'd brought me. "I thought humans were modest like fae."

"Many of them are, except when they're at the beach."

I pulled on the light blue bottom piece. It was shaped differently than Riku's. Mine covered a little more, like somewhere between underwear and short pants. The top was a little tricky. It tied around the neck and back.

"Oh dear," Riku said, examining me.

"What is it?" I looked down at myself.

"The top is a little small." She reached forward to readjust the fabric. "Well, I guess that will have to do. At least your nipples are covered."

"It's more than I would be wearing if this was a werewolf beach party," I commented.

"That's true," she laughed.

Riku went on ahead to search for the others since I had to wait for Konner to change. I exited shortly after her.

"Hey, Konner, you can change —"

The raw lust that came through the bond knocked the wind out of me. Konner stared at me, astonished, like someone had just slapped him.

I sucked in a deep breath and held it for a moment. Then I let it out in a rush and tried to get control of the situation.

"Konner, you can go change now." I tried to sound like I hadn't noticed anything, but I doubt I was convincing.

He nodded but didn't move or take his eyes off me.

I opened the door and gently pushed him toward it, ignoring the feel of him under my hands.

The movement seemed to wake him a bit, and his face turned red as he shut the door behind him.

While he changed, I pulled my shirt on over my swimwear and tried to forget Konner's reaction to me. I was somewhere between glee and scolding myself when he emerged.

The glimpse I'd seen of Konner when we'd arrived in Imani had been enough to tease me into untoward thoughts. But at the sight of him bare-chested and standing with pride as if inviting me to look, my thoughts became downright wicked. I knew they were wrong and forbidden and, if acted upon, would bring both of us to ruin. I didn't care.

I pictured his face contorted in pleasure as I milked every ounce of magic out of him. I saw my hands in the shining copper threads and my mouth on every inch of exposed, and unexposed, skin. In my head, I nibbled and licked his ear. My breath was hot in his ear when I said, "I love you."

The fantasy crumbled to dust as the words echoed off the walls of my mind.

Konner still stood there without embarrassment or any clue of my life-changing realization. And as I met his deep brown eyes, I promised myself he never would. *I will protect you even from myself. You will awaken and gain all of your magic. Because I love you, I promise you this.*

I turned from Konner and headed up the beach. His confusion at what he'd missed passed through the bond while he shadowed me without a word. I was relieved when we reached the rest of the group as it was easier to pretend everything was normal.

While we'd been gone, the others had arrived. They greeted us cheerfully.

"Nice touch, Runa," Raven complemented my over-shirt. "Humans sometimes wear just a shirt over their swimsuits."

I was glad to have an excuse to keep my shirt on, but Konner pouted in disappointment.

With everyone there, the party started. We all headed to the water for a swim. As everyone else laughed and splashed, I stood apart in the shallows, contemplating what I should do.

Maybe it would be best if I unbound from Konner and left. If he stayed with his aunt, he would probably be safe until his awakening.

Then I thought of my vow not to leave him until his awakening, the attack that had nearly killed Wilhelm, and the pain my leaving would cause both of us. I sighed.

I'm too much of a coward to leave him anyway. Besides, he only has a little over three months.

I watched him laugh and play for a while, feeling bittersweet.

Three months. Then I have to let him go. He'll go down whatever path he chooses, and I'll join werewolf society.

Even though the thought made me miserable, I didn't long for the rational attraction I felt for Keir and Rowan. *My love has manifested in an impossible form, but at least I know what it feels like. Not many werewolves are blessed enough to feel the joy and agony of love. I'm lucky.*

I knew it was a good time to commit to the future, to make a decision about with whom I would mate and what I would do. Making the decision would cement my resolve. But as I watched the sunlight glisten off Konner's wet hair and skin, I knew I wouldn't do it with him around. *Coward.* The only resolution I could make was to revel in what little time we had together. I knew it would only hurt more later, but it would be worth it.

The rest of the afternoon was like a dream. We played, ate good food, and had a bonfire. As the sun drifted toward the western horizon, it was time to go.

"We should get back before dark," I told Konner through the bond.

He stood with me to leave.

"I'll return your swimsuits next week," I told Riku.

"You can keep them. They're too big for us anyway."

"Thanks."

After saying our goodbyes and thanking them for inviting us, we began walking home.

"*Everything all right?*" Konner asked. "*You've been a little strange today.*"

"*It's all new to me,*" I answered vaguely.

"*Yeah, but it was fun,*" he said, misinterpreting.

I smiled over at him.

He reached out and grabbed my hand as we walked.

I'm sure to regret this later. I kept my hand in his.

A letter addressed to me waited on the messages table. Konner's eyes glinted with curiosity, but he didn't ask as he went upstairs to wash.

I took the letter to the study to read it undisturbed.

Dear Runa,

How are you? Are you enjoying Imani? I can't believe it's been two weeks since I saw you last.

We're fine here in Yarinbel. We spend a lot of time at Byron's warehouse, where the Fireleafs send the herbs they grow for packaging and distribution.

While I'm glad being away seems to have separated Wilhelm from the attack, I wish we all could have gone to the same place.

These weeks without you have made me under-

stand a lot about how I truly feel. I…well, I will tell you more about that when I see you again.

Don't forget me.
Rowan

My chest tightened as I read Rowan's eager words. *What am I supposed to do?* Closing my eyes, I sighed heavily as guilt crept into my heart.

Konner fell asleep early that night, exhausted from a full day of fun and fresh air. I stared at him in the dark, imagining caressing his face and his warm body close to mine. I didn't fall asleep for a long time. When I finally awoke, it was afternoon.

"Feeling better?" Konner asked as I entered the second floor sitting room.

"Why didn't you wake me?"

"You were tired. Besides, I wasn't going anywhere."

I sat beside him casually, needing to be near him.

"What're you thinking and feeling right now?" he asked.

"What do you mean?"

"I feel as though you've been blocking certain emotions from me recently."

"Not at all," I lied.

"You don't have to shelter me, Runa. We're in this together."

"Some things are private. Don't you have things you want to keep to yourself?" I knew he did.

He was silent for a while. Finally, he couldn't hold it in. *"Like thinking about your potential mates?"*

"Something like that."

We both stewed in our own misery.

"You don't have to hide it from me." Konner was a glutton for torture.

Yes, I do, I said to myself.

We both moped for the rest of the day, wanting to be near each other but incapable of being as close as we really wanted.

That night, the space between our beds felt like a canyon. We lay awake in the dark as the distance between us became like a weight on my chest.

I climbed out of my bed and crossed the room to lock the door. I knew every step closer to Konner would be a knife in my heart later.

He was surprised when I got into his bed, but he didn't say anything. He just moved over to make room for me. Though we were very close, I tried not to touch him, afraid of what would result.

Every night for the two weeks that followed, I slept in Konner's bed. Sometimes he'd have erotic dreams about us, and I'd pretend like I hadn't seen. Any dreams I had were, mercifully, kept to myself, having practiced blocking since Konner saw my dreams of Mikhail.

One morning, before leaving to go to the university, we found a letter for Konner on the messages table.

Dear Konner,

I hope all is well in Imani. I've heard good news from the matchmaker. She has found another potential mate for you. Please meet her this Saturday at Ashem's Café at one in the afternoon. Her name is Kenna.

Good luck!

Love,
Mom

All the lighthearted joy and hope for the future disappeared from Konner's eyes. He decided not to go to the university that day. Instead, he anxiously wasted time around the house, switching between periods of lying motionless and moving restlessly toward no set task.

That night, I held his hand as we lay in bed, trying to provide comfort. *"Konner, are you still planning to get mated like your parents want?"*

"Probably…most likely…possibly…perhaps…yes."

I would've laughed at his answer had the situation not been so serious.

"That's your decision. But, it seems to me, we won't be here much longer. And if you've decided to mate and stay on the farm, shouldn't you enjoy your time here while you can?"

He sighed. *"You're right."* He squeezed my hand and went to sleep.

The following day, we returned to the university.

"We thought you left without saying goodbye," Riku said, frowning at the prospect.

"We just had some stuff to work out," Konner explained.

"We're going to the human realm to see a movie this weekend, so I can get you that book, Runa," Ezio promised.

I smiled at him. "Thank you, but be careful. Won't you?"

Ezio nodded. "Of course."

"Do you want us to bring you anything, Konner?" Raven asked.

"Do you think you could get a postcard of where you're going?"

"Sure thing." She smiled.

"We'll tell you all about the movie, too," Riku vowed.

"I look forward to it," Konner said, like it was

the only thing that would get him through the weekend.

When Saturday dawned, both Konner and I were reluctant to leave his bed. He slowly moved his fingertips up and down my arm. Normally, that kind of caress would get my fire burning. But, that day, it was the only thing keeping me from bursting into tears. *The man I love is going to meet a potential mate today, and I have to watch.*

It made me feel only slightly better to know he'd rather stay in bed with me.

As time stubbornly continued forward, we had to leave the comfort of his bed and go forth to meet our fate.

As good as Konner had looked when he'd met Raina, he looked even better to meet Kenna. He wore a thin, short-sleeved shirt that clung to his muscular chest and arms and light blue jeans that made me want to take them off.

"Are you ready to go?" he asked.

I nodded. *No.*

The café where we were to meet Kenna was near the depot. Though the walk was short, it took a while. Our heavy hearts slowed our feet.

There weren't many people at Ashem's Café. I might have enjoyed the artistic atmosphere had I not been there for such a heartrending purpose. Ivy grew on the awnings above the paned windows. Inside, the scent of coffee and pastries hung among the outlandish yet tasteful paintings. The entire back wall was a bookshelf, packed with used books. Its size dwarfed the small round tables and twisted metal-legged chairs.

We approached a fae woman with dark red hair,

who looked like she was waiting. She glared at us, her mouth a rigid line.

"Are you Kenna?" Konner asked.

"I am, and you're Konner?"

He nodded, and we sat at her table.

"It's nice to—"

"Cut the chat," Kenna interrupted Konner's pleasantries. "Let's get this straight: I'm only here because my parents have not agreed for me to mate the one I love. You and me? Won't happen. Got it?"

Konner and I held our breaths in surprise as warmth spread to our chilled hands.

"Your parents too, huh?" Konner laughed without mirth.

Kenna's eyes widened and then squinted at Konner suspiciously. "You aren't interested in mating me?"

Konner shook his head. "No offense intended. My parents have expectations contrary to my desires."

"I know the feeling," she said bitterly. Then she smiled at us, blushing slightly.

"So why won't your parents let you mate the one you love? If you don't mind me asking."

"Ryuu is not their type. He isn't your stereotypical masculine man, and they don't approve of his endeavors."

We stared at her, slack-jawed.

"Does this Ryuu study human technology at the university? Sister Riku? Both petite?" I asked.

Kenna's fingertips covered her parted lips. "You know him?"

We nodded. "We met a few weeks ago at the bookstore and have recently become friends."

"Then you know how kind, thoughtful, and intelligent he is." She smiled into the distance.

Thinking of our initial reception, I couldn't help but think Kenna was Ryuu's exact opposite. However, she was obviously passionate about her feelings for him. *Way to go, Ryuu.*

"How did you two meet?" Konner asked.

"Not long after I had awakened, I took a trip to the capital with some friends. There was an exhibit on human culture at the museum. Ryuu's mother and father were there as guest lecturers for an event. While walking around the exhibit, I stopped in front of a picture on the wall. Ryuu saw my interest as he happened by and explained the photograph was of a rocket launch. I was so enthralled by his explanation that we ended up spending the entire afternoon together. We met every day until my vacation was over and I returned home. Then we exchanged messages and met when we could. Eventually, Ryuu asked me to be his mate, and I accepted. But within ten minutes of meeting my parents, they refused him. They think humans are lower than animals and said Ryuu was weak and unfit. But my heart is already his, and I will have no one else."

Her story of love and heartache resonated deep within me. "Is there any way we can help?" I asked.

She shook her head. "I don't think so."

"Well, for now, you can tell your parents that I refused you because I'm in love with someone else."

My heart leapt into my throat.

"Is that true?" Kenna asked.

"Does it matter?"

"I suppose not, but they'll just find someone else."

"Stay strong. They can't hold out forever. You love each other, and so few of us get that in our lives. They can't really force you to mate someone else."

She nodded, resolved.

"How's Ryuu taking all of this?" I asked.

"He promised to wait for me for as long as I still want him, but I can tell their disapproval hurts him."

"Shower him with love. That's all the strength he needs," Konner advised.

She gave us a light smile, her clear eyes sparkling. With renewed courage, she said goodbye.

"I really hope it works out for them," I said on the walk home.

"I'm going to tell them, Runa. When we get home, I'm going to tell my parents I want to go to a university."

I laced our fingers together as we walked, showing him my support.

The following week, Konner looked toward the future with determination. He even picked up an application for admission from the university and thought seriously about different emphases in human studies.

I was glad to see him working hard toward his goal, and I was sure his parents would support him.

The human studies majors had enjoyed their time at the movie in the human realm. They were all excited about 3D technology and special effects, whatever that meant. Apparently, the movie they'd seen was a remake because they argued about the positive and negative attributes of it compared to the original. Raven brought Konner a movie poster that had a drawing of an all-white character with a red circle around it and a line through it. The words at the bottom asked, "Who you gonna call?"

Ezio presented me with *The Complete Works of William Shakespeare.*

"He's considered the greatest writer of the English language. It may be difficult to read at first, but we speak a dialect of modern English. Be aware, though, humans don't speak like Shakespeare anymore," Ezio informed.

"Thank you," I said to Ezio as he handed me the heavy book.

Later that week, as Konner and I lay in his small bed, I watched him in the lamplight. The flame from the lamp revealed his copper strands in an alluring tease that remained just out of reach.

It took all my self-control not to run my thumb along his slightly parted lips. My own skin prickled with sensitivity, begging him to touch me, but he didn't hear the call.

"What do you want to do for Treaty Day?" Konner asked, pulling me from my fantasies.

"I don't know. Whatever you want."

"Well, what have you done in the past?"

"Mikhail and I never really celebrated together. I mean, we didn't exchange gifts or anything. Usually, his parents had a dinner party."

"He never gave you a Treaty Day gift even though you were his bondmate?"

"No, but I never gave him a gift, either. It's not like we wanted to be bondmates, and I learned not to press the issue early on."

"Do you not want to do anything with me then?" He sounded disappointed.

"Of course I want to celebrate Treaty Day with you. I

was just explaining I had no ideas because I've never cele-brated it before. My very first time will be with you, Konner."

He flushed with pleasure, and I smiled.

"Every year at this time, I'd imagine what we would do together if you were with me."

"Then you choose. I want to make your fantasies come true."

It was dangerous and teasing to use such suggestive language with Konner, but the filter on my brain couldn't handle the sight of him at the moment. Keeping a lid on my desire was starting to get painful, and that was the only way to release it I would allow myself to do, if only a little.

But Konner's answering blush just made me want him even more.

"What do you want to do, Konner?" I whispered aloud.

He swallowed hard. "I uh…what?" His eyes searched my face for guidance.

"For Treaty Day, what would you like to do?" I put him back on track before I really did something I shouldn't.

"Oh um, yeah…Treaty Day. Well, there is a festival going on at the harbor. We could go to that."

"Is that what you want?"

"It sounds kind of fun."

"Okay, let's do that then."

He smiled but still looked distracted by other thoughts. I know I was certainly distracted. There were so many things I said and did to him in my head, but I never moved. I controlled my actions even when I had no control over my urges.

24

A few days later, Konner awoke excited about our first Treaty Day together. He couldn't wait to leave the house and go to the festival. I was just happy to have Konner to myself for an entire day.

I was surprised the summer heat didn't deter people from being outside, but the sea breeze provided some relief.

The wide road near the harbor was packed with stalls and games. Bondmates of all ages smiled and laughed as they ate and played together.

Konner and I strolled among the colorful banners and cheerful festivalgoers. The smells from the various food stalls mixed into a complex, but pleasant, aroma. Children screamed and chased each other, and we smiled at their joy.

As always is the case when werewolves are together, there were all kinds of competitions.

"Do you want to enter the games?" Konner asked as we passed the entry booth.

The games poster listed a number of events to compete for the title of "Best Bondmates" in different age groups.

"It seems a little unfair to the rest of the teams, doesn't it? I mean, we're clearly the best bondmates."

Konner laughed.

We turned to walk away when a nearby werewolf in human form met my eyes with a challenge. He wore a mocking expression that said, "You *should* walk away because no one can beat me."

"You know what? Let's show them what well-matched bondmates can really do," I told Konner aloud.

We signed up, and I grinned a challenge back at the werewolf who'd mocked us. His eyes gleamed with anticipation as he and his bondmate strutted toward us.

"You think you have what it takes to beat us?" he teased when they'd reached us.

"I know we do." I grinned, enjoying the competitiveness.

He returned my smile appreciatively. "I'm Mick, and this is my bondmate Hudson." He held out his hand, and I grasped his outstretched forearm.

"I'm Runa, and this is Konner."

"Good luck to you both."

"Keep it for yourself." I smiled. "We don't need it."

He barked a laugh. "This is going to be fun."

Konner was happy I was enjoying myself. Though not as competitive as his brother, he seemed pumped to win.

The competition had three trials. The first was a test of strength, speed, and teamwork. Each faeling tied a sash around his or her waist in such a way that, if pulled, it would come off. Whichever team could steal the other faeling's sash won and moved on to the next round.

We competed against a male werewolf and his female bondmate. He was strong, much stronger than I was. But I was quicker.

As guardians, the other werewolf and I automatically moved to protect our faelings. We circled each other as our bondmates looked for openings. The female faeling advanced a few times. I was able to block her, but her bondmate engaged me before I could get her sash.

"Konner, follow my lead and try to advance, but let him block you. I'll stop him before he can get your sash."

"Okay."

"Konner, follow me," I said aloud. I moved left, and Konner followed, advancing only to be blocked. We did that a few more times, creating a pattern of expectation.

"Okay. This time, go the opposite direction. I'll try to occupy him so you can get her sash."

"Got it."

When I went right, Konner went left. By the time the guardian realized what had happened, I'd already launched myself at him. Thanks to my speed and momentum, I was able to tackle him to the ground. "Oof." We landed in a pile.

The maneuver gave Konner enough time to snatch the faeling's sash, and the bell rang at our victory.

As I detangled myself from my opponent, his body shook with laughter under me. I offered him a hand up, and he let me help him to his feet.

"You're serious, aren't you? I'm not going to complain though. It isn't every day I get tackled by a pretty girl." He smiled good-naturedly and went to his bondmate.

"You should've punched him instead." Konner glared at his retreating back.

I tried not to laugh. *"That wouldn't have been very sportsmanlike."*

He harrumphed, and I smiled up at him.

"Good teamwork," I congratulated.

"That will only make our victory all the sweeter," Mick chimed in before Konner could respond.

"Keep dreaming," I taunted back.

He chuckled and winked at me.

"These guys are going down," Konner vowed.

"Agreed."

The second test was to see how strong the bond was.

The three remaining wolves stood behind one of three curtains, and our bondmates had to choose which curtain we were behind. After every choice, we shuffled around behind the curtains for the next faeling to guess.

When it was Konner's turn, I could feel him searching the bond. He found me without any problems. Unfortunately, Hudson easily found Mick, and we both advanced to the final round.

The last test was to see how developed the bond was. The judge would secretly ask the fae a question. The bondmates had five seconds to write what the fae was feeling. If the answers matched, the team won.

The judge stepped up to Konner, and I could

hear what she asked through Konner's mind. *"How do you feel when you're with your bondmate?"*

Arousal shot through the bond, and I froze. *I can't write that.*

I was about to ask Konner what he'd written through the bond, but the bell rang. Our time was up. The judge looked at our papers. Mine was blank, and Konner's read "happy."

That's one word for it. I met his eyes, and an enticing blush colored his cheeks. *And I'm not much better.*

Mick and Hudson won the title of "Best Bondmates" without issue. They approached us afterward with smug smiles.

"Go ahead. Praise me," Mick demanded.

I tried not to be a bad sport. "Good job, guys. You really are well-matched."

Mick's smile turned sulky. "It's not fun if you're going to be nice about losing."

I shrugged.

"What happened anyway? I watched you in the first trial. Your bond is definitely in the telepathy stage. Empathy should've been no problem."

"I guess I couldn't find the right word."

My explanation seemed to satisfy him. Before the conversation could go on any further, I grabbed Konner's elbow and steered him away. "Well, have fun at the rest of the festival. Congratulations on your victory." I smiled and waved as we walked away.

"Are you sure you don't want to hang out with them? Mick seemed...interested in you."

"Nah, that's just how male wolves are sometimes. Besides, I came here to spend the day with you."

He was pleased by my response and smiled cheerfully.

"Are you hungry? Do you want to get food?"

"Sounds good. Let's go."

We ate tons of different kinds of food until our bellies were full and happy.

When we strolled through the merchant area, I remembered that I hadn't gotten Konner a gift.

"Konner, I haven't bought your gift yet. If you shop with me now, do you promise not to peek?"

"You don't have to get me anything, Runa."

"But I want to."

"Okay, I won't peek if you won't."

"Deal."

It was difficult to shop with the person I was buying a gift for and not ruin the surprise. Luckily, the shops and stalls were crowded and carried a variety of goods.

After we'd discreetly purchased our presents for each other, Konner suggested we find a quiet place to exchange them.

We walked a while before we found a deserted dock to exchange our gifts.

"Close your eyes," I told him, and he obeyed.

I took a soft, auburn-colored scarf from my bag and touched it to his cheek. He smiled and opened his eyes.

"I know it's summer right now, but it'll be cold again before we know it. I don't want you to catch a chill."

He smiled lovingly at my hurried justification. "I love it, Runa. Thank you."

I sighed in relief and smiled self-consciously back.

"Your turn. Close your eyes."

I did as I was told. He gently pulled on my hand so I'd hold my arm out. I felt him wrap something firm around my wrist and fasten it.

"Okay," he whispered, his voice quivering.

I looked down at my wrist and saw a cuff bracelet of dark brown leather with two buckles fastening it. I touched the supple leather and beamed up at him. "Thank you, Konner. It's beautiful."

"Not as beautiful as you," he let slip through the bond.

I didn't let on that I'd heard him even though I glowed inside.

"You're welcome. I'm glad you like it."

The setting sun shimmered on the water and revealed the copper in Konner's hair.

"Should we head back to your aunt's?"

"But the best part of the festival is after dark."

"Isn't that dangerous?"

"Awakened fae and adult werewolves are standing guard so we can enjoy the festivities. Also, this is Imani. Nothing is likely to happen here."

I was still a little reluctant, but I found myself nodding under his pleading gaze. He led me to a park nearby where the festival was held.

All the streetlamps and house lights had been put out in the area around the park. Little orbs of glowing pink light floated among the trees, illuminating a field of grass at the center of the park.

I gasped with delight, and Konner grinned at me. *"Do you like the fae lights? Once I awaken, I'll make them for you."*

"That would be wonderful." I smiled as my heart sank.

As the sun dipped below the horizon, bondmates started to gather in the clearing. A fae with a large basket went around to all the faelings and gave them small bells on ribbons. Konner took his and tied the ribbons around his ankles. When everyone was ready, the faelings formed a circle in the middle of the clearing. A slow drumbeat sounded, and a flute sang from somewhere unseen. As the faelings started to dance, swaying their arms, the bells on their ankles chimed.

I stared as Konner spun and leapt in a coordinated fae dance. His powerful legs glided gracefully in time with the others. He was bewitching, and I wanted nothing more than to take him right there in the open field.

"Are you ready?" Mick asked me, shattering my fantasies.

"Ready for what?"

"For the wolf dance." He grinned.

Shortly after, the drums beat harder and faster, and the faelings cleared the space.

Mick motioned for me to follow him into the circle. As the sound of the drums called to my spirit, I joyfully joined the wolf dance. Unlike the graceful spins of the fae, we jumped, stomped, and howled with wild energy.

I'm sure it wasn't much to look at, but it was fun. Unfortunately, it also got the blood pumping. When I'd located Konner once the dance was over, he stared at me with the same lust I was feeling.

Uh-oh.

Thankfully, before either of us could do something stupid, an awakened fae approached us and offered to take us home.

I was disappointed to leave the enchanted meadow, but it was probably for the best with us both feeling so raw.

Our walk was short and deafeningly quiet. Our escort tried to make conversation, but Konner and I were wrapped up in our own thoughts. We thanked her and went inside to bed.

It took a long time for sleep to take me. I was too aware of Konner's warm body, ready, willing, and well within reach. The images of him dancing in the glowing meadow were fresh and sweet, and featured heavily in my dreams that night.

25

A few days later, we received a message from home giving us the all-clear to return. The following day, we went to the university to say goodbye to our friends.

Konner said he hoped to return one day to study with them. When I said goodbye to Ryuu, I told him, "Trust in your love, Ryuu. You'll be together soon."

He smiled and nodded, eyes filling with grateful tears.

That night, Konner made a special dinner as thanks to Keyri and his aunt.

"It's going to get boring without you two around," Keyri complained.

"I guess you'll have to come visit us on your next break," Konner suggested.

"You bet I will. I have to teach Wilhelm all of my wild ways."

"I don't think he needs your help," I added, and everyone laughed.

"Are you ready?" I asked Konner as we lay in bed. He nodded. *"It's long overdue."*

"Don't worry. I'm sure they will understand, and I'll be with you the entire time."

The small depot in Konner's hometown was crowded with returning faelings and their bondmates. Even though we'd been given the all-clear, I was still on high alert as we walked back to the farm. With every step, Konner steeled himself for the confrontation ahead.

We arrived just as Kat was setting lunch on the table. Everyone was so excited to be reunited that they rushed to embrace us. Rowan was the first to reach me. He lifted me into a spinning bear hug, his ice-blue eyes sparkling with joy.

"I missed you," he whispered and stepped aside so the others could hug me, too.

I felt guilty in the face of Rowan's elation, and I was glad Kat hugged me before I could respond to him.

As we ate, we told everyone about our visit and how Naiha and Keyri were faring. After lunch, Wilhelm and Rowan went to the library to catch up on schoolwork.

"Mom, Dad, do you have a minute? I have something important to talk about," Konner said as Kat and Ed cleared the table.

They looked at each other with wide eyes.

"Sure, Konner," Ed replied, motioning for us to sit at the table.

They gazed at him expectantly, and he hesitated.

"I'm with you, Konner," I reassured.

"I know you want me to find a mate and work on the farm after I awaken, but that's not what I want to do. I want to go to the university and major in human studies, and I'm not interested in being mated right away."

They stared at him, dumbfounded. The silence was palpable.

Finally, Kat's eyebrows pulled together, and she said, "I don't understand. I thought you wanted to stay on the farm."

Konner shook his head.

"Have you really thought this through? How long have you wanted this?" Ed asked.

"Ever since I started learning about humans."

"We thought that was just a hobby. Why haven't you told us until now?" Ed wondered.

"I didn't want to disappoint you," Konner admitted.

They scowled at him like he should know better. Sitting silently, they processed the information a while longer.

"I'm sorry, Konner. We're just a little shocked since this is the first time we're hearing about it," Ed said.

Konner nodded his understanding and kept his impatience and apprehension in check.

"Are you sure you've thought this through, Konner?" Kat asked.

"I'm positive."

She bit her lips and wrung her hands. "How about a compromise? Meet one more mate candidate. If you don't like her, then we'll find someone from the service to help you through your awakening. And you can go to the university and study whatever you like. If you do like her, then you will be mated and stay on the farm or go to the university together if you want," Kat negotiated.

Konner considered her proposal and nodded. "That seems an agreeable arrangement."

Ed and Kat rose from the table, still in a daze.

"Mom, Dad, thank you," Konner said, hugging them in turn.

"We want what's best for you, Konner, but we also want you to be happy." Kat patted him on the cheek.

After they'd left, Konner let out a huge sigh and turned to me, smiling. *"You were right, Runa. I should've listened to you sooner."*

"I'm happy for you, Konner." I grinned back at him as fear nibbled on my mind. *Trust him. He's intelligent and capable. He'll be able to protect himself when the time comes.*

Exhausted, we retreated upstairs to our respective rooms to unpack.

I managed to avoid Rowan until we went out to check the perimeter that evening. Every time I looked into his ice-blue eyes, I felt guilty. I knew he felt the same as before I went to Imani, and I was the one who'd changed. Facing his affection made me feel like I was taking advantage of him.

Being in wolf form made it easier to interact with him, and it felt good to stretch my wolf limbs in the open space of the farm.

As before, there was no hint of vampire scent. Before I went inside, I strained my ears, listening for howls in the distance. I heard only the normal sounds of a summer evening.

As expected, Rowan visited my room when our

checks had been completed. I made sure I was fully dressed before letting him in.

He smiled charmingly and stopped himself from reaching for me.

At least he remembers our agreement.

"I'm so glad to see you again. I missed you."

"Did you learn anything more about the vampires who attacked us?" I asked, moving the conversation to a business topic.

"Yeah, I looked into it when we arrived yesterday. The Wolf Council sent a team of investigators to sweep the area, but they didn't find a lot. The investigators think some of the vampires may have escaped into the human realm. They waited for the scent to clear and to see if they'd return. There's been no sign of them since the attack, which is why they signaled the all-clear and called everyone back."

"Do you know who the wolves who helped us were?"

He shook his head.

I nodded thoughtfully. "It's getting worse. The governments may have to revisit the treaty if one werewolf isn't enough to protect one faeling anymore."

"Are you all right, Runa?"

"Of course."

"You seem…different, and your scent is a little off."

"I'm rather tired from a long day, and I'm sure my scent still smells like the sea air."

"I like it. It suits you. So did you miss me?" His normally ice-blue eyes were warm like tropical waters.

"Of course, I missed everyone."

He cast his eyes down at my answer.

"I'm sorry, Rowan. I really am tired. Do you mind if I turn in early?"

Rowan's brow wrinkled in concern, but he left me to rest.

Of course, after saying I was tired, I couldn't go downstairs and read with Konner. Instead, I tidied the room, which didn't take long. With nothing else to occupy me, my mind started to wander.

I can't keep this up with Rowan. He deserves better. At the very least, he deserves to know I have feelings for someone else. It's only right that he should know what he's getting into should he still wish to be my mate. But won't he want to know whom? Maybe I should just give up on Rowan. If Keir won't have me, I can find someone new altogether. I might even be able to fall in love again.

My heart ached at the thought, and I pictured Konner smiling down at me. *I guess it doesn't matter. I was approaching mating as a rational decision before Konner. I'm sure I can see it that way again.*

The thought of mating someone else made me nauseated. I pushed the problem aside and took out the book Ezio had given me.

"Runa?" Konner called through the bond.

"Yes?"

"I didn't know if you were asleep yet. Rowan said you were tired."

"I'm still awake."

I bit my lip, knowing what he wanted but unsure of what to do. I could feel his loneliness as he lay in his large bed alone. My own bed was cold and too big without him in it.

I climbed out of bed and crept soundlessly to the

door that led to Konner's room, and I absolutely knew it was the wrong decision. He didn't say anything as I crawled into the empty space that awaited me.

We both relaxed a little, releasing the tension that our physical separation had caused.

It was a lot easier to sleep within reach but without touching in Konner's bed compared to the tiny beds at his aunt's.

My body was tired from arising at dawn after the previous weeks of sleeping in. But by the end of the week, I was used to waking up and doing chores again.

I managed to avoid Rowan's prodding for a few days. But as time passed, he became more and more concerned. One evening, after our perimeter check, he demanded an explanation.

"Runa, you're really starting to worry me. Please tell me what's wrong." His tropical water eyes swam with anxiety.

I sighed in defeat. "Rowan, I have something I need to tell you, but I'm not sure how to say it."

He took my hand gently in his, and I allowed it, knowing that what I said next would be a blow.

"Tell me as best you can. I'll listen."

His expression, so full of concern and affection, made me hate myself for destroying it. "While I was in Imani, I fell in love with someone. It's impossible. He and I can never be together, but I don't feel right not telling you."

Rowan looked like a kicked puppy: sad and lost and wondering what he'd done to deserve this. "Oh."

His eyes lost focus, and I couldn't decipher his expression.

"Why is it impossible?" He didn't sound like he really wanted an answer.

"It just is."

"And…you're still considering me as a potential mate?"

"I'm not sure I deserve to."

"To be honest, I don't know how I feel right now. Can I have time to think about this?"

"Of course."

"Thank you." He pulled away and closed off his normally easy-to-read expression.

After he'd left, I felt worse than I'd expected. I took comfort in Konner's bed and wondered when the right thing had started to feel bad and the wrong thing had started to feel good.

26

When Kat had announced the following morning that Konner's last match would be visiting that day, Konner nodded diplomatically and promised to give her a chance. I was confident Konner would find this one just as unsuitable as the two prior, and he'd finally be able to move forward and pursue his dreams.

Everyone else anxiously awaited her arrival. Konner paced the library wearing straight-legged jeans, a button-down shirt with the sleeves rolled up and a hunter green waistcoat. If I hadn't known better, I would've thought he was trying to attract this potential mate.

I was certainly distracted by the way he looked as he walked. I rested my cheek in my hand, appearing as though I was reading the book on the table in front of me. In reality, I watched Konner and imagined the things I wanted to do to him but never could.

I was convinced my thoughts were my own until

I felt Konner's arousal through the bond. Surfacing from my fantasy, I realized Konner was looking at the dark-haired beauty in the doorway of the library.

She tucked her straight hair behind a pointed ear as her hazel, woodland eyes sparkled at Konner. She strode toward him and held out her hand in greeting. He took in her form-fitting pants and sleeveless shirt, and then he shook her hand with an answering smile. I relaxed my jaw when I realized I was clenching my teeth.

"It's nice to meet you, Konner. I'm Arete."

"Welcome, Arete. I hope your trip was enjoyable."

"It was. Thank you. It's nice to be outside in the fresh air on such a warm, sunny day."

"Perhaps you'd enjoy sitting outside then?"

She smiled at him. "I'd like that."

Kat was bringing in cool tea as they left through the front door. She could hardly contain her excitement that they'd made a good first impression.

"Don't follow them too closely, eh Runa?" she whispered as I went along to protect Konner from potential threats.

What does she expect me to do? Leave him unprotected? Well, the threat is low at this time of day, and Arete has her magic. Plus, Konner did a pretty good job of fending off vampires when they attacked us.

Fighting the urge to stick close, I gave them a little privacy, but not so much that I couldn't hear their conversation as they sat in a sunny patch of grass.

"No, we don't have big open spaces like this where I'm from. Palendeen is mostly dense forest.

The sky looks so big here," Arete explained, grinning wide.

"What does your family do?" Konner asked, clearly interested.

Exploring the bond, I discovered he felt intrigued and was in a pleasant mood. I was surprised by his reaction but told myself it was good he was getting on well with a potential mate.

"My family studies magic. We look for better and new ways to help fae through advances in magic."

"That sounds interesting."

"It is. And your family grows medicinal herbs? My father swears by your herbs. He won't buy from anywhere else if what he needs is grown on your farm."

"Thank you. He does us great honor. But I'm going to go to a university for human studies after I awaken."

"Really? I don't know much about humans." Her laughter was too pleasant sounding, and Konner smiled. "My older brother used to tell me scary stories about humans when I was young, so I haven't been as interested as I might've been. Tell me, are they really as horrible as he said? They don't cut off little fae's toes and wear them as jewelry, do they?"

Konner choked on his laughter. "No wonder you weren't interested. How horrifying. Your brother sounds like quite the troublemaker."

"He is." She smiled fondly.

The longer they talked, the more at ease Konner became. *This is good for Konner.* I knew it was true, but it didn't ease the knot in my stomach as I watched them laugh and talk. While I'd accepted that I was in love with Konner, I knew he could never be my mate. Therefore, I wasn't going to act when my werewolf instincts urged me to challenge her and rip her pretty throat out.

As their conversation turned toward the issue at hand, I took a few steps back. I told myself I was just going to talk with Rowan, who was walking toward us, but I knew that wasn't true. Having muzzled my wolf, I was too much of a coward to listen any further.

Rowan explained that he'd been sent by Kat to see how it was going. He was distant as he talked to me, but he didn't avoid my eyes. In fact, I was worried his ice-blue eyes saw too much.

"Everything seems to be going well," he commented.

"Kat will be pleased," I reported.

Arete let out another musical laugh. I couldn't hear all of her words in this form, but I did pick out "mate" and "love."

My stomach lurched with unknown possibilities. Rowan watched me with eyes that were too sharp.

Konner and Arete seemed to have come to some sort of an agreement because they stood and moved toward us.

Could they have agreed to mate so soon? This was meant to be only the initial meeting. Then again, Konner asked me to be his bondmate during our initial meeting.

I could only tell that Konner was pleased, but I couldn't pinpoint the exact cause. I followed them to the road.

They smiled at one another as they shook hands.

"It was nice to meet you, Arete. I look forward to seeing you again."

"As do I. See you in two weeks."

She waved at us as she started her journey home. Konner waved back and went inside to face Kat's enthusiastic inquisition.

"So what do you think of her?"

"I like her. She's intelligent and full of life. She's returning in two weeks so I can show her around town."

I was already moving up the stairs when Kat asked, "What about a potential mating? Did you talk about it?"

"We talked about it—" Konner's words were cut off as I shut my bedroom door.

I repeated my new mantra. *This is good for Konner. They seemed to get along very well, and she certainly is beautiful. It's a healthy choice for him. I'm sure she's perfectly wonderful and will make him very happy.*

My wolf squirmed inside me, wanting to take action, but I knew her anger was really born of fear and despair. I curled onto my side and stared at the wall next to my bed. I knew what I told myself was true, but that didn't stop my heart from aching. I held up my hand and pictured it stroking Konner's soft, copper strands. My hand blurred as my eyes filled with tears. I squeezed them shut and eventually fell asleep.

onner came to fetch me for dinner, but I declined, telling him I didn't feel well.

He was concerned. "Do you want me to bring you anything?"

"No, thank you. But tell Rowan to come get me when he's ready to check the perimeter."

He promised he would and left me to rest.

By the time Rowan knocked on my door, my head was on straight. I'd censured myself for being foolish and vowed to do what was best for Konner. *Not only is that my job, but how can I say I love him if I can't do what's best for him?*

Our perimeter check was efficient and didn't end in our usual play-fight training session. I was disappointed, but I didn't blame Rowan for pulling away until he made a decision.

After returning to my room, I threw myself onto my bed. My gaze wandered until it fell on a book on my desk. *The book that describes the awakening ceremony.*

I wasn't prepared for the images of Konner and

Arete "becoming one" that writhed in my mind. I lay with my eyes squeezed shut, feeling miserable and trying to chase unwanted images away.

"*Runa?*" Konner called.

I panicked, thinking perhaps he'd seen or felt something I couldn't keep to myself. "*Yes?*"

"*Aren't you going to come to me?*"

My heart leapt with the desire to run to him, and I squashed it without mercy. "*I'm still not feeling well. I think I'll stay here.*"

"*Oh, okay. I hope you feel better.*"

"*Thanks. I'll see you in the morning.*" Don't listen to me, Konner. Please come to me.

I slept fitfully that night, tormented by my imagination and the fact that Konner never came.

The week that followed was rough. Rowan remained distant and formal. I didn't return to Konner's bed, and I didn't sleep well as my heart and body called for him in the night. I buried my emotions a little more each day, and the distance between us that resulted was making Konner worry. At the end of the week, Konner cornered me in the library and demanded answers.

"What's going on with you, Runa? Why are you pulling away and blocking me?"

I floundered for a reasonable answer and found none. "It's for the best."

"How can that be? Did something happen? Did I do something wrong?"

"No, I just…"

Rowan cleared his throat as he entered the room, and I realized we'd been having our conversation out loud. "Runa, you have a visitor in the sitting room."

Thank goodness! But who'd be visiting me? I assumed my guest would be Elva or someone else from the pack coming to check on me.

Fiery-blue eyes smiled at me as Mikhail stood to greet me. My mind went blank, and I'm sure my mouth hung open.

"Mikhail…what are you doing here?" I finally managed.

"It is so nice to see you again, Runa. I hope you have been well."

Fury shot through the bond as Konner glared at Mikhail with unveiled hatred. He looked as though he might lunge at any moment. I took in the two hulking wolf guards, who'd escorted Mikhail, and placed a reassuring hand on Konner's arm.

"It's fine, Konner. Let's just calm down and hear what he has to say."

Mikhail squinted his eyes ever so slightly at my hand on Konner's arm. No one else could see it, but I could tell he was annoyed.

"I'm sure you're very busy with your awakening and mating a few weeks away, so why don't we skip the formalities. Tell me why you're here, Mikhail."

"Please, Runa. We know each other better than that. Call me Mika."

My eyebrows shot up at him inviting me to call him by his shortened name as he'd always insisted I not be so familiar with him. Konner bristled.

"Why are you here, *Mikhail*?" I repeated.

"I always liked how straight-forward you are." He smiled charmingly.

I didn't respond but waited for him to get on with it.

"Could we speak alone please?" he asked, flicking his eyes at Konner.

"Absolutely not," Konner raged.

Mikhail raised his eyebrows at me, waiting for my answer.

"You heard him."

"Very well. I was only trying to spare his feelings"—he stepped close to me, and Konner and I both tensed—"Runa, I miss you, and I want you to come home."

Out of all the things Mikhail could have said, I never would've guessed it would be that. Shocked isn't strong enough to describe how I felt.

Konner grabbed Mikhail by the collar and pulled him in menacingly. The wolf guards shifted their weight to attack, but Mikhail held up a hand to halt them.

"You listen to me, you twisted son of a bitch. Runa isn't bound with you anymore. She's *my* bond-mate. You can't mistreat her or order her around ever again."

"I have said some unforgiveable things to Runa in the past. That's why I'm here to make amends. Do you really believe you can provide for her better than I can? Besides, it isn't your decision. Runa, please, come home with me."

I put my hand gently on Konner's arm to get him to release Mikhail. He let go, and Mikhail straightened his clothes.

"Runa, you can't—" Konner started, worried.

"Mikhail, I'm glad you repent your mistakes, but I'm bound with Konner. You have plenty of people to protect you. Konner needs me. If it's my forgiveness you want, then you have it. I know you only lashed out at me because of the pain of losing Isla. I wish you well in the future, but I'm staying here."

Mikhail hadn't expected for me to turn him down. His expression was truly pitiful.

"Please, Runa," he begged. "You don't understand. I *do* need you. My parents were furious when they had discovered I had been unbound without their permission. They said it looked bad as if they'd abandoned the orphan they'd saved. They told me that taking you in was the main reason Colleen's family had agreed to allow her to marry below her. I've been trying to find you for months before they find out and break our engagement. Please, Runa, I need your help to save my future. I'll give you anything you want. Konner can even come and stay with us so he's protected."

I felt sorry for the situation Mikhail was in even if it was of his own making. I knew he really wanted to mate Colleen, and his offer wasn't unreasonable if Konner would be safe.

Konner's emotions were all over the place: anger and pity but mostly fear. Fear of losing me, and fear of being abandoned and alone again.

Even if Mikhail's proposition was reasonable, I could never betray Konner like that again. "I'm sorry, Mikhail. I hurt Konner once. I won't do it again."

Mikhail's eyes flashed, and he sneered at Konner. "What is so great about you? Why would she choose you over me?"

"Because I love her," Konner meant to say to himself. I pretended I didn't hear and that it didn't thrill me. "Because we're well-matched. We were

meant to be. Don't forget, Mikhail. It was *you* who stole her from *me*."

Mikhail scrunched his face in disgust and left without another word.

Not two seconds passed before Konner embraced me. He thrust one hand into my hair at the base of my neck and wrapped the other arm around my waist to hold me to him. I buried my face in his chest and breathed in his scent. I allowed myself to take comfort in him if only for that moment. I knew Arete still loomed in the background, and my actions would only make it more difficult for me later. I didn't care. I felt Konner's warmth and listened to his heartbeat.

"Thank you," he whispered.

No, Konner. Thank you.

Our embrace took its course and broke naturally. Though my body mourned his distance, I told myself not to let it happen again. *It's not right. Nothing can come of it. If he isn't already promised to another, he soon will be.*

Our emotional trial inevitably bridged the distance that had been growing between us, or at least that's what I wanted Konner to believe. Maybe I was becoming a better actress or maybe I liked punishing myself, or both. Either way, I'd told him nothing was wrong so many times that I seemed to have fooled myself into believing it. However, I still didn't sleep beside him. Mercifully, he didn't call for me and was too embarrassed to ask why I didn't come to him. I offered no explanation.

28

*A*rete returned a week after Mikhail's surprise visit. She and Konner both seemed excited to tour the town. I, of course, had to join them. To my surprise, Rowan and Wilhelm also accompanied us.

"The more the merrier." Arete smiled when we met her at the depot. She chatted happily with Konner and Wilhelm as Rowan and I followed behind.

Not surprisingly, Wilhelm seemed to like Arete as well. He laughed and teased her like she was already part of the family, and she teased back like an older sister.

I concentrated on protecting Konner and tuned out their conversation, though sometimes her musical laugh slipped through my blockade. I was careful not only to school my expression under Rowan's watchful eyes but also to emotionally detach myself from the situation. I blocked out everything Konner was feeling, leaving only enough room to pick up on fear in order to gauge potential danger.

Under the circumstances, the situation was a lot like when Mikhail was courting Colleen. I was to remain vigilant to threats but silent and out of the way. In a way, the familiarity was almost comforting.

My armor felt flawless until Konner smiled and laughed with her. Then my wall crumbled and my raw nerves were exposed. I reacted quickly to rebuild my defenses before any of his feelings could leak through, or mine could leak out.

We walked all over town as Konner and Wilhelm pointed out the sights to Arete. The towns-people stared, of course, but this time Konner's future mate was the center of their attention. I was relieved that their eyes, at least, were on her and not me.

Even without the bond, I could tell Konner was excited to show Arete Zen's shop. Before we entered, Wilhelm and Rowan excused themselves to run an errand for Ed. They promised to meet back at Zen's when they were finished.

The bell above the door tinkled as we entered.

"Wow!" Arete exclaimed. "All of this stuff was made by humans?"

"That's right." Zen smiled, appearing from a back room.

"Arete, this is my friend, Zen. It's his shop."

"Nice to meet you, Zen."

"Konner, you seem surrounded by beautiful women. Hello again, Runa."

Arete laughed at his compliment, and I raised my hand in greeting. Something caught Arete's eye, and she went to explore. Konner followed her, and I approached Zen.

"How are you, Zen?"

"I'm well, thank you. I'm sorry to say you've looked better. Is something wrong?"

I sighed. *I guess I wasn't as convincing as I thought, or Zen is very perceptive.* I took in Zen's concerned expression and answered truthfully. "I'm feeling as though Konner would've been better off if I'd never returned."

He watched Konner and Arete trying on human hats as they laughed and made faces. "I don't think so. You didn't see him before. He's changed for the better since he was bound with you."

"Really? How?"

"Would you like me to show you?"

"What?"

"I can use a spell to share a memory of Konner with you."

"You can do that?"

He nodded.

"But who'll protect him in the meantime?"

"It'll feel as if you're gone for a while, but in reality, it will only be a few seconds."

"All right."

He smiled and said a phrase in ancient Elvish. Then he reached two fingers toward me and touched me lightly on the forehead.

The bell chimed to warn me a customer had arrived.

"Kat, Konner, welcome. How can I help you?" I smiled.

"I have errands to run, Zen. Do you mind if Konner stays here while I take care of things?"

"Sure, and don't worry. Our wards were just updated."

"Great. Thank you. Konner, I'll be back in a little while. Stay here with Zen, all right?"

The bell tinkled as Kat left. And thus, I was left with the sullen youth.

Konner always arrived at my shop in a bad mood. But after a while, amongst the things that interested him, he usually came around.

"I've got some new photographs, Konner. Would you like to see them?"

He didn't answer, but he drifted toward me. I pulled a photo album from the shelf and put it on the counter. He leaned his elbow on the glass and flipped through the pages. His guarded expression gradually smoothed into contentment.

"How old are you now, Konner? Fifteen?"

He nodded. "I'll be sixteen in a few weeks."

"You're getting close to your awakening then. Don't you think it's about time you request a bondmate?" I asked in a curious, nondemanding way so he wouldn't take it as a challenge.

He looked up at me with wide eyes as I'd never broached the topic before. His eyes shifted back to the counter. He reached out and picked up a key with a seven-pointed star and a crescent moon on it. He turned the key over in his hand, watching it catch the sunlight that filtered through the window.

"She'll come back," he said quietly but with confidence. He silently played with the key for a while, then continued. "I know she misses me as much as I miss her. She can't be happy bound with someone else."

"Will you tell me about her?"

He smiled to himself. "She's kind and generous. She's trustworthy and honest. I'm sure it was her sense of honor that led her to being bound with someone else. She wouldn't abandon me unless it was really important. But she will come back to me. I just know she will."

I wasn't sure whether he was trying to convince me or himself, maybe both.

I smiled at him. "I'm sure you're right. She sounds wonderful. I'd love to meet her. Will you bring her to the shop when she returns?"

Based on his look of astonishment, he wasn't used to people believing his claim that his lost bond-mate would come back. He smiled gratefully and nodded.

Zen's smile replaced Konner's as I returned to the present. Konner and Arete were still trying on hats.

"What did I tell you?"

I nodded to him. "Thank you." My voice was thick with emotion. *Zen's right. Konner is better because I came back to him.*

While Zen's memory made me love Konner even more, it also cleared my head. *I'll live up to Konner's faith in me by ensuring his future happiness. If he wants Arete, I'll support them.*

I clutched the copper key around my neck, a reminder of Konner's image of me that I must live up to.

I squared my shoulders and knocked down the wall to Konner's emotions. He certainly was having fun, but I couldn't be sure if he wanted to mate Arete. He found her attractive, but no lust was present at that moment.

I'll have to ask him later and be ready to help in any way I can.

As the afternoon wore on, Rowan and Wilhelm came to fetch us from Zen's shop. We walked Arete to the depot so she could go home.

"Keep in touch, won't you?" Arete asked outside the depot.

"Of course, I'll write you."

She smiled and hugged Konner and Wilhelm goodbye. Then she waved to Rowan and me and entered the depot.

Konner and Wilhelm recapped their day with Arete on the way home as if we all hadn't been there.

"She'll make a good mate," Wilhelm said after a while.

Konner nodded, and my heart sank. No matter what I promised myself, it would be difficult to watch the one I loved mate another.

29

After dinner and the perimeter check, I found Konner in the library.

"Konner?"

He looked up from his book.

"Do you mind if we talk in private?"

He laughed. *"We are talking in private."*

"I mean where we won't be interrupted."

He closed his book and nodded, and then we went to his room.

He sat on the edge of his bed, and I stood facing him.

"So have you decided when you and Arete will be mated?" I steeled myself for his answer.

His eyebrows squished together. "Didn't you hear? Arete and I aren't going to be mated."

"Huh?"

"I told everyone after her initial visit. We're only friends. I thought you were there when I said it."

"I thought…"

"She came to visit because she wanted to see our town and Zen's shop."

My heart felt so full it would burst. "But why? If you both like each other enough to be friends, why wouldn't you mate? I...I know you were attracted to her, and she seemed to be attracted to you."

He blushed and remained silent until he could collect his words. "She wants to mate for love, and I'm...unavailable."

I almost choked on my own heartbeat. The room suddenly felt too small, and Konner seemed very close at a step away.

He stood and took that step into my personal space. My mind told me to move away, but I gazed up into Konner's warm eyes. My breath caught as he reached up and tucked a stray lock behind my ear. He ran his thumb along my jaw.

"Runa," he whispered like a prayer. "You must have noticed."

I couldn't move, couldn't speak to respond.

"I know it's impossible...I know you could never...Runa, I love you." He held his breath, terrified at what my reaction would be.

"Konner, I...I love you, too."

He couldn't believe what he'd heard. He stood, transfixed, but my words eventually sank in. "Are you...is this real? Is that why...is that why you didn't come to me over the last two weeks?"

I nodded sorrowfully.

When he cupped my face and leaned toward me, my whole being wanted nothing more than to go where he would lead. Instead, I halted his advance with a hand on his chest. My stomach churned with his pain and confusion, so I hurried to explain.

"We can't. It's already gone too far. We've broken the rules as it is, but I will not take your magic."

"I'll give up anything for you."

"I won't let you."

He saw my resolve, so he didn't press me. He slowly caressed the side of my neck and ran his fingers through my hair. Pulling the ends of my long, white hair gently toward him, he pressed the soft tips to his lips. *I don't think I'll cut my hair after all.*

I wondered if he'd meant the gesture to be as erotic as it was.

"Promise me," I panted, fighting both of our desires. "Promise me, you won't sacrifice your magic. Promise me you'll awaken."

"But Runa, don't you know that means I have to…become one with someone else." My stomach churned with his nausea.

"I know, but it's the only way." I unsuccessfully tried to hide my own misery.

"What will happen to us?"

I couldn't meet his eyes when I responded. "You'll awaken and go to the university like you planned. We should try to enjoy the time we have left." I let the insinuation hang in the silence.

He couldn't let it drop. "And what about you?" He didn't want to hear my answer, but he needed the truth.

"I will…join wolf society and choose a mate."

"No," he protested, knowing it was the only way.

My throat closed around an emotional lump. I didn't try to speak, afraid to show a crack in my resolve.

"Is it…will it be with Rowan?"

I answered honestly. "I don't know."

My jaw ached as Konner clenched his teeth together at the thought of me mating Rowan. It seemed to upset him more than if it had been some faceless, unknown werewolf.

"What should we do now?" He was lost, and I wasn't much better.

"The best option would be for us to forget this conversation ever happened, to let our feelings go, and to distance ourselves from each other until you awaken."

"I can't do that. Even if I could, I wouldn't."

I smiled sadly. "Neither can I. The only option that remains is for us to treasure the time we have left without sacrificing your magic. Your parents will hire a guide from the service to help you awaken, and then…then we have to let each other go."

His face twisted in despair as the truth of my words sank in. He hugged me close to his chest, and I clung to him. Sharing our mutual sorrow didn't make it feel better, but it somehow made it easier to bear.

Our desperate embrace stoked my desire to be as close to him as possible, but I didn't allow it to escalate. *I failed to keep my feelings to myself, but I will not sacrifice his future.* Even with my resolve at the front of my mind, it didn't stop my body from reacting to Konner. His strong arms held me against his firm body, and I could feel his arousal not just through the bond.

I took a shaking breath and broke contact. "We need to be careful," I warned.

He nodded his understanding and reached out his hand. I took it in mine, and we sat on his bed.

"Do you regret it?" I asked through the bond.

"What?"

"Any of it: my being your bondmate, my returning, you loving me, my telling you that I loved you."

"Not one bit." He smiled his adoration. *"Even if it's forbidden, and we can never really be together, I'm grateful I fell in love, and I'm glad it was with you."*

"When did you know you loved me?"

"I think I've always loved you. I just didn't understand at first. And when you came back, you were even more beautiful than I'd remembered. I was really surprised by my reaction to you. But when did I know I loved you for sure?" He thought about it for a moment and even his inner voice sounded mournful when he answered. *"I knew when I saw you and Rowan kissing."*

"Oh." I shifted my eyes to our entwined hands.

"Are you really going to mate him?"

"I really don't know, and I don't think I should talk with you about it. It will only upset you, and it's not your decision to make." I tried not to sound mean, but I still needed him to understand.

He sighed heavily and nodded.

"I saw your dreams, you know."

He flushed and feigned ignorance. *"What dreams?"*

"The ones where we were together."

He met my eyes, then looked away, embarrassed.

"The night I stayed with you after Rowan and I...that night was the first one of that type I saw. You really did grab my breast you know, and I enjoyed it."

The shift in conversation successfully distracted

him from talking about Rowan. The lump in his throat jumped as he swallowed.

"Is uh…is that when you knew you loved me?"

"No, I knew I loved you that day at the beach. You didn't make it easy for me to hide my feelings either. I could feel your lust every step of the way."

"I suppose I was pretty bad."

"Seriously, I thought I'd die the time I cut my finger. I had so many wicked thoughts."

He smiled at the steamy memory. *"But I didn't feel your attraction through the bond."*

"I'm just better at blocking. I've had practice as a bond-mate, remember? But, oh, the things we did in my fantasies."

His lack of experience didn't allow him to understand the many possibilities I referred to. Still, he got the basic idea.

"I'd sacrifice my magic for one night with you."

"Don't say that."

"I'm serious."

"So am I. You will awaken, won't you? Konner, please promise me you will," I begged.

He reluctantly met my pleading eyes. *"I promise."* He paled, and my stomach dropped with his.

I raised my free hand to his face and placed it on his cheek *"This is what's best for you."*

"If you say so. But I'm only doing this because you want me to."

"Thank you."

I stood to go to my room for the night.

He tugged on my hand so I'd look at him. *"Don't go."*

"I'm not sure it's a good—"

"Please. We have such little time left, and I've promised I will awaken. Stay with me, Runa."

I couldn't fight myself and him. We crawled into his bed and stared at each other in the candlelight from his bedside table. As before, we kept our touching to a minimum.

"I love you, Konner," I whispered as his eyes drifted closed to sleep. His lips twitched into a small smile.

30

I felt a lot lighter after Konner and I had confessed to each other and set a future course. Even though we only had a little over two months left together, at least I didn't have to pretend around him. We seemed the same well-matched bondmates to everyone else, but we shared our love freely through the bond. The only outward change in behavior was that we spent a lot more time in our rooms rather than the library. In reality, we were in Konner's room, where we could touch and show affection openly. It was difficult to keep our physical desires under control, but with such little time, we were happy just to be together.

Though Rowan had seemed distant, he hadn't stopped paying attention.

"You're in a better mood recently. You were melancholy before," Rowan pointed out as we mounted the stairs to shift for our nightly patrol.

I was relieved that he'd noticed only a change in my mood.

"I am. I may as well enjoy the present for the future is uncertain and probably bleak."

He seemed surprised by my outlook but not displeased.

In the weeks that followed, Rowan slowly warmed up to me again. It started with him going out of his way to greet me and ask how I was. His mask-like features softened into more expressive reflections of how he felt. Eventually, he began to play with me again. It had been a while, so I lost the first couple rounds. His victories elated him and brought us even closer. After a few weeks, our relationship was almost back to normal. The one aspect that was different was that he was more territorial. He hovered around me and used any excuse he could to touch me familiarly.

I understood why. *Because he views me as a potential mate, his wolf instincts are telling him to reinforce a bond between us and ward off competitors.*

I knew he couldn't help it, but his behavior was noticed. Kat watched us with a twinkle in her eyes, and Wilhelm made a few pointed jokes. Konner, on the other hand, was much less thrilled. He fought the urge to bring up how much it upset him because I'd told him it wasn't his business.

One evening, I entered the library where Konner, Wilhelm, and Rowan sat reading. As I looked for a place to sit, I saw a chair was missing.

"What happened to the other chair?" I asked.

"Mom needed something sturdy to stand on while cleaning earlier. I think it's in the hall," Konner informed me.

I moved toward the door to retrieve it, but Rowan stopped me by grabbing my wrist. He pulled me onto his lap. "You can sit with me, Runa. I don't mind sharing."

"Ooooo," Wilhelm cheered.

Konner's face turned purple as rage charged through the bond. He slammed his book closed and left the room.

Rowan didn't care at all. "Was that crossing the platonic line Konner drew?"

I gave him a look that said he knew it was, and he grinned like I'd slapped his wrist.

He let me go without resistance, and I followed Konner to his room. He didn't answer when I knocked, but I went in anyway.

Konner paced the floor with long, angry strides. *"Konner —"*

"I can't do this, Runa. I can't watch Rowan put his hands on you. I can't touch you, but you never stop him. I keep imagining the things he'll do to you if you're mated. It hurts. It hurts so much."

I knew exactly what he meant because I'd seen the same things with Arete. I moved toward him slowly to attempt to comfort him though nothing I could do would ease this pain. The images would arise every time he saw Rowan and I together.

He stopped pacing and hung his head in defeat.

"I'm sorry. You have a right to future happiness. He… Rowan will make a good mate."

"I'll talk to him again." I used the back of my fingers to wipe away a tear, which had escaped down his cheek.

He snatched my hand and pressed his lips to my palm. His breath was hot and wet on my skin, and his lips were as soft as butterfly wings.

Desire shot through me, and I knew he felt it

through the bond. I was wrestling it for control when he traced his lips along my hand and licked the tip of my finger.

My composure broke. I wrapped my hand around the base of his neck and pulled him down to me, crushing his lips with mine. He responded eagerly, pressing our bodies together. His firm chest and abs burned me through our thin, summer shirts. He kissed me so thoroughly that I had to break for air. I gasped as he kissed down my throat. I was trailing my hand down his stomach to reach under his shirt when he whispered, "I love you."

It was like a bucket of cold water. I stilled my hand and let it drop limply to my side. Konner noticed the change immediately and stopped.

I grabbed his hand and placed it on my cheek. "I love you too, Konner. That's why we have to stop."

We were both stretched thin. I cleared my throat and indicated toward his erection, which fought bravely for freedom from his pants. *"That could get painful if you don't take care of it. Why don't I come back in a bit?"*

He blushed, and I tried not to laugh. *Fae are so strange sometimes.*

The memory of Konner pressed against me, and the knowledge that he was on the other side of the door thinking of me as he stroked himself, was enough imagery for me to satisfy myself quickly.

"Runa?" he called when he had finished.

"Yes?"

"I'm uh…you can come back now."

I opened the door that led from my room to his and leaned against the door jam.

"That was too close, Konner."

"I know." My face heated with his shame.

"I feel like we're bound to fail if we stay on this path."

"I shouldn't have started it. I was feeling self-conscious about Rowan, and I just needed to know you want me."

"It wasn't only your fault. I was an all-too-willing participant. I should've had more control. Of course, I want you. That's the problem...I think we should separate ourselves physically, starting with sleeping in our own beds."

His disappointment joined mine in the bond.

"Please don't. I won't do it again. We have less than two months left. Please don't sacrifice any time we have left together."

"Do you think I want to?"

"I'll be good. I promise."

"But will I?"

I gave in to our longing and crawled into his bed beside him. He was careful not to touch me.

"Thank you." He smiled sweetly.

Could he be more of a temptation?

he next morning, Rowan asked me to meet him by the spring after we had finished with the chores. I agreed, thinking it would be the perfect time to talk about boundaries. I sat in the shade and watched the fish swim lazily in the cool, clear water.

When Rowan approached, I stood and smiled a greeting. He didn't return my smile, but looked at me with pity. *Is he going to turn down my suit?*

"Runa, what are you doing?"

I looked down self-consciously. "What do you mean?"

"The person you fell in love with, the impossible mate, he's Konner. Isn't he?"

My throat closed in panic, and my mouth dried up. I could only stare at Rowan, terrified, as he explained.

"When you had said you fell in love with someone in Imani, I was sure it was a wolf of a much higher class. While I was hurt, I still wanted you. But how could I be certain he wouldn't come for you? He could've mated you if he wanted to, and I couldn't imagine he wouldn't. You were so miserable when Arete came. I thought seeing them court only reminded you of your far away love. I was a little surprised when you still watched them sorrowfully even after Konner said they were only friends, but then you recovered. You were lively and joyful again, and I thought maybe you'd let go.

"When you had said the future looked bleak, I assumed it was because I was distancing myself from you, and you thought I wouldn't be your mate. I was so happy to think you wanted me that I started treating you like my promised. You seemed content with the idea, and you didn't push me away. So I came to your room late last night, while everyone else was asleep, to ask you to be my mate. I was worried something had happened to you when you weren't there, but then I saw the door that led to Konner's room was cracked. When I looked in, everything made sense."

"Are you going to turn us in?" I whispered, holding my breath for his answer.

He eyes were heavy with sadness. "No, I won't tell anyone, and I know I don't have to tell you it's forbidden. Please listen to me. You need to stop this now before it's too late. If anyone finds out, you'll both be cast out. And what about Konner's magic?"

"I know," I sobbed.

He placed a comforting hand on my shoulder. "You can't help who you fall in love with."

I gazed into his eyes and said what I'd been thinking for a while. "It would've been so much easier if it was you, Rowan. But you're right. We can't control who our hearts choose."

He smiled bitterly. "I feel your pain, but be smart, Runa. You should break it off. It will be better for you both."

"There isn't anything to break off. We both know that, after he awakens, we have to let each other go. He promised to awaken, and I won't let him sacrifice his magic. So nothing will happen. I even told him I'll be mating another wolf."

"No wonder he was so pissed at me."

"You don't have anything to worry about, Rowan. We both know it's impossible, and we accept it. We're only trying to enjoy what little time we have left. I was in Konner's room last night, but we were only sleeping."

"Handling it that way will only make it worse later."

"I know, but I can't help it."

His eyebrows pulled together in sympathy, but his eyes clouded like he really did feel my pain. "Will you let me help you?"

"How? There isn't anything anyone can do."

"I can pick up the pieces when this is all over."

"Don't you want to find love for yourself?"

"It's too late for that."

A sadness I couldn't comfort or conceal filled my heart. "Oh Rowan, no."

He nodded seriously. "I realized while we were in Yarinbel."

Guilt gnawed at me.

"It'll be a while before Wilhelm awakens, but maybe by then you'll have room for me. Runa, will you be my mate?"

My heart broke for him. "Rowan, I'm already lost, but you don't have to give up. Besides, if I agree, you'll see me as your promised. How would you handle watching Konner and me for the next seven weeks? Your instincts would drive you mad."

"Just as you can't control your heart, neither can I. Please. I know what I'm signing up for. I know it will be rough, and it will hurt worse than any pain I can imagine. But I can endure seven weeks of watching you love another for a lifetime with you. I know we can be happy together. We get along. We have fun. I know you're attracted to me. Most importantly, I know the truth, and I accept you anyway. Let me take care of you, Runa. Once we are unbound, we can be free together. We can travel like you wanted and fill your heart up with happy memories."

His speech was certainly convincing, but I was still reluctant.

"I don't deserve you."

He smiled at me. "It doesn't matter because you have me. Runa, you can lean on me. Let me help you. I want to soothe your aching heart."

"Will you promise me something?"

"Anything."

"If you should meet another wolf who you fall in love with, will you promise to break it off with me? I can't stand the thought of me keeping you from someone you love."

"Can't you just keep something for yourself for once? You're too kind, Runa. I seriously doubt that will happen, but thank you for being so considerate. I promise."

He stepped close to me. His eyes were warm tropical waters. "Runa, will you be my mate?"

"I will."

He leaned down to seal our agreement, and I resisted the urge to squirm. *Rowan's right. This is my best option. It wouldn't be right to mate Keir while I love Konner, and I will have two years to become someone Rowan deserves.*

His lips brushed lightly against mine, and a new bond was formed. It wasn't a telepathic or empathetic bond like my bond with Konner. It was a bond between wolves. Our wolves accepted each other as equals and would attune to each other. He was my pack and, as soon as my bond with Konner was broken, Rowan would be the most important. He would be everything. But, at that time, I felt aware of him, and a little tug told me to keep him near. It wasn't like the longing my love for Konner made me feel. But, once we were free of our fae bonds and fully mated, our instincts would take over, and the tug could easily grow into a need.

He smiled down at me, feeling the wolf bond. "That feels nice."

To me, it felt confusing. My wolf wanted to be close to Rowan, but my heart cried for Konner. I'd never been at odds with myself. "Will you let me talk to Konner before we tell anyone else?"

He nodded seriously. "Do you want me to go with you?" he asked, already protective of his promised.

"No, it'll be better if I go alone. Besides, Wilhelm is probably wondering where you are."

Our arms brushed together as we walked back to the house. I quickly discovered that my wolf's nervousness only felt soothed when I was touching Rowan.

Rowan found Wilhelm in the library, and I went in search of Konner.

He'd just gotten out of the bath and was toweling his hair dry as he walked to his bedroom. His scent was warm and clean, and droplets of water dripped onto his shirt. As I followed him into his room, his smile was welcoming. He held out a hand to tell me to come to him, but I stayed a few steps away.

"Did you talk to Rowan? You were gone for a while. Did he take it badly? I felt your distress through the bond, but I thought it was best to let you handle it."

I nodded and tried to organize my thoughts. *"I talked with Rowan, and we've come to an understanding."*

His eyebrows shot up at my formal tone, but he waited for me to continue.

"I've agreed to be his mate once you and Wilhelm have awakened."

My stomach churned with his nausea. *"Why did you have to choose him?"*

"I didn't have to choose him. He was the best choice. He knows I'm in love with you, and he still accepts me. That's practically unheard of."

He sucked in air. *"You told him?"*

"I told him when I'd returned from Imani that I'd fallen in love with someone because he deserved to know. He figured out it was you on his own."

"What does this mean for us?"

"Nothing will change until after you awaken. Rowan's agreed not to tell anyone about you and me and to muzzle his wolf until then."

"What do you mean 'muzzle his wolf'?"

"*There are certain instincts that go along with being around your mate or promised. He'll try to keep them under control.*"

He unsuccessfully tried to hide his despair.

"*I'm sorry, Konner. I wish it could be different.*"

He sighed and pulled me into a tight embrace. "*I know. Me too.*"

32

*E*veryone else was overjoyed about Rowan and me. Kat even called for a special treat. She wanted to make a feast in celebration. Because the next few weeks would be dominated by the first harvest, she agreed we should wait until that was finished.

Though I spent every night with Konner, Rowan didn't say a word. But there was still tension between them. I showered Konner with love when we were alone, which was a lot of the time. Of course, we remained within the boundaries of our physical relationship, still unwilling to risk his magic for a blissful yet brief moment.

The tug my wolf felt toward Rowan grew a little every day. We often sat close together, only realizing it when Konner got upset. The harvest kept us all busy, so Rowan and I didn't have much time together, which only made my wolf more anxious. I could tell Rowan's wolf resisted his shackles, but he did a good job of keeping him under control. Sometimes, he'd snap at Konner or touch me familiarly to show the competing male that *he* was my choice.

Of course, it made Konner furious, but it couldn't be helped. Knowing that the same instinct had resulted in many wolves' deaths, Rowan was actually doing remarkably well.

Konner and I tried not to fight since our time was quickly running out. As a result, a distance was growing between us again, formed and fueled by our unexpressed frustration. It was completely natural for both Konner and Rowan to be jealous, but Rowan already knew he would win in the end. There was no point in Konner or me talking about it or getting upset, but I could tell Konner's resentment would explode eventually. I did everything I could think of to delay the inevitable outburst.

"Konner?" I called one night as we lay in bed.

He grunted but didn't look at me.

"I love you."

He sighed. *"I know."*

I moved closer to him, not enough that we were touching but close enough that I could feel the warmth of his skin.

"Do you know?"

"Yes."

"I don't think you do. I can't do any of the things I want to do to you. But I can show you if you can handle it without finishing while I'm here. Can you hold out?"

His head snapped toward me, and he nodded while holding his breath.

"Tell me if it becomes too much, okay?"

I opened the bond to show him one of my many fantasies…

I walked to the bathroom for my morning bath and opened the door without knocking. Konner had been lifting his shirt to take it off and jumped when I barged in. His face flushed with embarrassment.

I didn't apologize for the intrusion; instead, I shut the door behind me.

"You don't have to be embarrassed in front of me, Konner, though that color is delicious on you. Please continue."

His blush spread to the tips of his pointed ears. I smiled at the effect and moved toward him. He didn't step away. When I'd reached him, I slipped my hand under his shirt. His abs were firm, and I trailed my hand up to his toned chest.

He helped me remove his shirt, and I pressed kisses along his collarbone to his throat. Then I brought his mouth down on mine. His kiss was insistent, and I let the tension build.

Our arousal, along with the steam from the bath, overheated me. I broke our kiss and stepped back, peeling my clothes off as his eyes, clouded in need, watched me.

When I'd returned to him, he reached for me hesitantly. I wasn't so shy when I dropped his pants and released his ready cock.

I took his hand and led him to the hot bath. Neither of us cared when the water spilled over onto the floor as we climbed into the large tub.

I leaned toward him and pressed my wet body to his. Even though the water was hot, I could still feel the heat of his skin.

His breath caught when I placed his hands on

my breasts, and I gasped as his thumbs rubbed my tight nipples.

I climbed on top of him, leading the tip of his cock to the brink of my core.

"Stop," Konner gasped, breaking the fantasy.

His face was red, and he panted heavily.

"I can't…I promised…"

I got up quickly and went to my own room. Even though I'd have to touch him while being emotionally connected for him to lose his magic, I thought it best not to risk the temptation. I wasn't confident I could restrain myself if he stroked himself within my reach, and I wanted so badly to feel him as we serviced ourselves in our separate rooms.

When I crawled back into Konner's bed, he felt better than before.

"Thank you for showing me."

"I want you to think of that every time you see Rowan and me together. That's how I feel. That's what I want to be doing. You are the one I love and want to be with."

This time when I said it, he knew they weren't just empty words.

When we'd finished harvesting the first crops, Konner, Wilhelm, Rowan, and I were charged with taking the ones that weren't being dried to the depot to ship to Byron in Yarinbel.

There were far fewer fresh herbs, and they were all able to fit in a decently sized handcart. It was still pretty heavy, so we each took turns pulling it.

After sending the shipment, we turned back

toward home. We weren't far from town when we heard rustling in the bushes near the road. Rowan and I swiftly moved between our bondmates and the sound.

Two werewolves in human form burst through the brush and moved around us to continue on whatever path they were following. The female's long, cream-colored hair whipped behind her as she ran. Her yellow eyes met mine for a fleeting moment, and I felt like someone had punched me in the gut.

"Isla?" I wondered.

She stopped in her tracks and turned slowly toward me.

"Runa?" She blinked rapidly with a furrowed brow, but she didn't seem dumbfounded like I was.

The male tugged on her hand. "Isla, let's go. We'll lose the trail."

She moved to follow him.

"Isla, wait!"

"Go home, Runa. I'll find you."

Then she disappeared into the brush.

We stood silently in place for what felt like hours.

Isla's...alive?

Eventually, Konner placed a hand on my shoulder. "Let's go home and wait for her there."

I walked home in a daze, not sure how long it took. It was as if I picked up one heavy foot, then put it down, and I was home.

After a lunch I didn't eat, I sat at the window in the library for most of the afternoon, watching the road that led to town. Konner and Rowan stayed with me. Konner read aloud to pass time, but I don't know what the book was about. Rowan remained silent but stayed close to me.

As evening approached, I finally saw Isla and her companion appear as they moved toward the house.

I jumped up from my seat, startling Konner and Rowan. They followed me as I ran out the front door. I sprinted toward her with my arms flung out, ready to embrace the friend who I'd been sure was murdered.

The sharp look in her yellow eyes made me stop short and drop my arms, but it couldn't stifle my joy and enthusiasm.

"Isla, I can't believe you're alive. I can't tell you how happy I am. What happened? How did you survive? Why didn't you come back?"

She stared at me seriously, and her sharp eyes shifted to Konner. "Not in front of him."

Everyone but her companion was taken aback by her demand.

"It's okay," I assured her. "Konner's my bondmate."

"I know. I can smell the bond all over you. He goes, or I do."

I looked back at Konner, unsure of how to proceed.

"I think I'll see what Wilhelm is up to. It was nice to meet you, Isla. I'm glad you're alive and well. Please let me know if you or your friend would like anything to eat or drink before you leave." Konner was the model of hospitality as he smiled and went back to the house.

"I'm sorry, Konner. I love you."

"I know. I love you too, and be careful."

33

*O*nce Konner was out of sight, Isla hugged me tightly.

"I'm so glad you're safe, Runa. But I thought you were bound to Mika. Why are you here with Konner?"

"It's a long story, but yours is far more important. What happened?"

"We have time for that once we get you both out of here. Come on." She grabbed my hand and pulled, but I wouldn't budge.

"What? We can't leave. Who will protect Konner and Wilhelm?"

"Who cares who protects them? They aren't your masters anymore."

"What are you talking about? Masters? They're our *bondmates*."

Isla looked helplessly at her companion, who shrugged.

"Fine, we'll do this the long way. What do you remember about the attack?"

"I remember your parents getting killed by vampires, and one of them drank you dry. I saw your limp body drop to the ground. My father covered us as my mother escaped with me. They were both killed as well."

She nodded. "The vampire that killed my parents did drink a lot of my blood but not all of it. Sometime after they chased after you and your mother, a group of wolves on the hunt found me. They were tracking the vampires who attacked us. They saved me from bleeding out on the road and brought me home with them."

"But why didn't you return once you recovered? And why didn't the wolves who saved you send word that you were alive to your intended bondmate?"

"They don't live like we were raised. They've found a better way. They aren't groomed from birth to serve fae. The pack is a family, and they protect and raise the pups until they reach full adulthood. They don't hand over their children to act as guard dogs for the fae. They're free to grow and mature, to fall in love and mate. The benefits of the treaty are in the fae's favor. Our realm of origin isn't as bad as they make it out to be. We can easily keep our identities secret as long as we follow a few simple rules."

Rowan and I were both stunned. What Isla described was so foreign to anything we'd ever known. It took a while to grasp what she said and form a coherent response.

"You live in the human realm?" The caution I'd been taught from a young age made me fear for Isla's safety. *Fae going to the human realm is one thing. They have magic to hide their presence. But werewolves? The only way for us to not be discovered is to stay in one form. With both forms being so integral to our existences, that's not even an option.*

"We live in *our* realm. Remember, werewolves originated there," Isla emphasized. "We have rules we have to follow, of course. But humans don't believe we exist anymore. As long as we're careful, we can live among them with ease. The society you and I were raised in is founded on our fear of humans for their past deeds, but the world isn't the same place it was centuries ago when we fled. There are many who want to keep things the way they are, so they propagate this culture of fear."

What she's saying seems plausible, but have we really been deceived our entire lives?

"I don't understand. If you live in the hu—realm of origin, why are you in Faerie?"

"Even though we aren't bound to fae, vampires are still our natural enemies. They prey on humans as well and make life dangerous for us. Our pack, and others, hunt them down and kill them. Sometimes, that means we follow them to Faerie."

"There's more than one pack?"

"Of course, but the Wolf Council and the fae certainly wouldn't want any werewolves in Faerie to know that. Once I recovered, I tried to get the pack to come back for you. They sent someone to gather information, but it was too late. You were already bound to Mika, and it would've been too difficult to get you out. But this is great; being bound to Konner means you can easily just leave with us through a nearby portal. You *will* come with me, won't you, Runa? You can be free, and you can mate your promised whenever you want. You won't have to wait until your bondmates awaken."

"How do you know Rowan is my promised?"

She smiled. "There's so much we can teach you. I can smell your matebond. It's faint, so it must be recent. Being raised with the pack means you learn to be a better wolf. My senses are a lot sharper than they were even in human form. I bet you couldn't smell that I'm mated to Misha." She indicated toward her stoic companion.

I sniffed and couldn't smell her matebond.

"See? I have so much to tell and show you. Please come home with me."

I certainly was tempted. I wanted to learn to be a better wolf, and I longed to be reunited with Isla. "If you're here, does that mean you were tracking vampires?" I asked.

"The vampires are getting bolder with the approach of the Blood Moon, and they've become confident since they started hunting in groups. I'm sure you know about the attack that happened here a few months ago. We've been hunting the culprits and caught most of them. But a few gave us the slip, and they regroup fast. We're positive they'll come back soon. Misha and I were following a trail when we came across you. It was probably too faint for you to smell it. The trail went cold before we could discover where the vampires went."

"A few months ago? On Midsummer? That was your pack who rescued us? I knew I smelled something familiar."

Her eyes widened. "I was so busy with the vampires. I didn't notice you were there."

"If you're tracking them, that means all the fae in this area are in danger. Why didn't you sound the alarm?"

"If we did that every time we smelled a vampire in Faerie, we'd spend all of our time howling. Besides, the trail was old, and the vampires were gone."

I looked at Rowan, and he appeared as worried as I felt.

"Isla, we can't go with you. If there are vampires around, we can't leave Konner and Wilhelm unprotected." *And I have so little time left with Konner as it is. I won't leave him before I absolutely have to.*

"But, Runa, don't you get it? They're using you. Don't you want to be with your own kind?"

Her words stung me, but I replied calmly. "I won't put Konner and Wilhelm at risk. Your offer sounds intriguing, but it will have to wait."

She frowned but nodded because I was at least interested in her proposal. "When will Konner awaken?"

"In five weeks." I felt sick even saying it aloud.

She looked at Misha, and he nodded. "I'll come back for you then." She turned to Rowan. "Think it over, too. I'm sure you don't want to wait to mate Runa. You could come with us as well."

Rowan seemed conflicted as he nodded his acknowledgment.

Isla hugged me again. "I've missed you, Runa. I hope you decide to join us. Should you want to meet us before I come for you, go through the portal near town and follow the path. Turn left at the cross-roads, and you'll find us." She rested our foreheads together and smiled at me. She was just as reluctant to leave as I was to let her go. "I'll see you soon," she promised. Then Isla and her mate bid us farewell and left.

It took all my strength not to chase after her. Rowan slid his arms around my waist, hugging me from behind. He didn't comment or ask me what I would choose. He just let his proximity ease my tension. We stood like that and watched them leave until they were out of sight.

"We should go in. Konner and Wilhelm are probably climbing the walls." I left Rowan's embrace, but the comfort he'd given stayed with me.

"What are you going to tell him?" Rowan asked as we returned to the house.

"The truth. You?"

"I'm not sure. The truth would probably be best, but maybe I should wait."

I knew the choice to go with Isla in five weeks would be much more difficult for Rowan. *He's torn between his desire to mate me and his promise to protect Wilhelm. I'm sure his bond with Wilhelm is warring with his bond with me.*

"Hey." I grabbed his arm so he'd stop walking and face me. "Even if I choose to go with them, you can stay until Wilhelm awakens. You don't have to choose between us. I decided to stay and protect Konner until he awakens, so I'll understand if you want to stay with Wilhelm."

"That's not the only reason you chose to stay with Konner," he said bitterly, knowing the whole truth.

"I won't deny it. I just don't want you to suffer, Rowan."

"No matter what I choose, I'll have to give something up."

"That's true, but you don't have to choose between Wilhelm and me. I already promised to be your mate. Whether it's in five weeks or a few years, I'll still be there."

34

Konner waited anxiously for me in his room. He rushed to greet me with a tight embrace.

"Are you all right? What happened?"

I silently let his comfort thaw any remaining tension. When I'd arranged my thoughts, I told Konner about how Isla had survived the attack, how her pack saved us, and her offer.

He was as surprised as I had been to hear about the wolf packs living in the human realm. After I'd finished, he hesitated before he said, *"You could've gone with her. I know how important she is to you."*

I nodded. *"I'm just happy to know she's alive. Yes, she's important to me but not as important as you. No one is as important as you. We don't have much time left, and I can join her later if I want."* I stroked his hair affectionately and smiled at him.

His answering smile didn't reach his eyes. He remained in his own thoughts until later that night. As we lay in bed, he finally let me know what was bothering him. *"Do you agree with Isla? Do you feel like a guard dog?"*

"When I first came here, I felt like I was helping a friend. Now, I'm protecting the one I love. No, I don't feel like a guard dog, not with you."

"What about with Mikhail?"

"Sometimes he treated me like a servant, so how could I not feel like one?"

"Maybe Isla's right then. Maybe fae got the most benefit from the treaty." He frowned at the thought.

"I don't know. There are definitely benefits for were-wolves to live in Faerie. Maybe the terms are just too strict? Perhaps bonding shouldn't be compulsory? On the other hand, werewolves who want to live in Faerie should have to contribute, right? Isla and her pack have found another way. Though I'm sure the Wolf Council doesn't encourage wolves to leave, it doesn't sound like they're trying to stop them either. I do think the werewolves of Faerie should be made more aware of their options. In any case, it's a compli-cated issue, so I don't feel asking 'are we guard dogs?' captures the whole question. That's why they try to match bondmates well, isn't it? So we don't mind being together for so long? So we want to protect our friends?"

"I guess you're right. It is a complicated issue."

"Regardless, I'm glad we're bondmates."

"Me too."

The following morning, Kat asked Konner to complete the form in order to request a guide for his awakening.

"I thought she said she was going to take care of it?" I asked as I read the form over his shoulder.

I regretted my curiosity after seeing questions like: Sex preference? Body type preference? Hair color preference?

My stomach dropped when I'd realized the questions were to help pick a guide Konner would be sexually attracted to. I ignored his embarrassment and left him to fill it out in private.

I found Rowan outside, chopping firewood. The look on my face made him put down the axe and move toward me.

"What's wrong?"

I didn't answer. I just wrapped my arms around him and buried my face in his chest.

He stroked my hair soothingly without saying a word. He knew exactly what I needed.

It wasn't right to seek comfort from Rowan when I knew he loved me, but my wolf sought him out in my time of need. However, when I looked up into his tropical-water eyes, my heart cried because they weren't the brown I wanted to see instead.

"I'm sorry," I said, stepping out of Rowan's arms.

"I don't mind."

"I know, but that makes it worse."

I turned to leave, but he grabbed my wrist. "Hey, I'm here for you. I'll hold you together when you go to pieces. Take comfort in me whenever you need, for whatever reason. Runa, please don't stop coming to me."

My wolf was happy to hear his words, but my heart broke even more for him.

As the bond of the promised grew stronger so did my sorrow. My wolf was pleased with her choice of mate, but I felt as though she was pulling me away from Konner. My heart longed for him even as my instincts wanted Rowan. Mostly, I felt guilty, guilty toward both Konner and Rowan.

Rowan deserved someone who would love him foremost, and I should've protected Konner by keeping my love to myself. All their suffering was my fault. By trying to live honestly, I'd hurt them. By trying to live morally, I'd hurt them again. I knew I was wronging them both, but I didn't know what else to do.

The cycle of warring with myself and feeling guilty for my choices tainted my time with both of them.

I never did see what Konner wrote on his form. But, a week later, I got a clue when a guide visited the farm. She had a similar build to me with long, blonde hair and blue eyes, as close to my white hair and light gray eyes as fae features could get. She seemed very comfortable with herself and sensitive to Konner's nervousness when she shook his hand.

"Hello, Konner." Her voice was soft and delicate, nothing like mine. "I'm Violet, and I'm pleased to make your acquaintance."

"Welcome, Violet." Konner's voice shook slightly, and his eyes darted to mine.

I couldn't bear to watch, so I excused myself and went outside. My pain made my wolf want Rowan, but I resisted the urge to take comfort in him.

She is beautiful. Should I be flattered that she looks as close to me as a fae can?

The wind was chilly as it rustled the leaves in the trees, which were just starting to change color for the season. The water in the spring was cold as I trailed my hand through it, but at least it distracted me momentarily from my thoughts and emotions.

I knelt on the smooth rock and sat on my feet, watching the fish drift around in their own peaceful world. Finally, I stood to stretch and go inside when my legs had fallen asleep and the chill had started to get to me.

Konner walked up the path toward me, and I meandered to meet him. I was stunned when he kissed me forcefully on the mouth. I could taste his agony as it mixed with his tears.

"I can't do it," he cried, crushing me to his chest.

I trailed my fingertips up and down his back to help him relax. I didn't respond for a long time, letting the silence and my embrace soothe him.

"Konner, you have to, and you can't fake it either. You have to trust her and become one with her in order to awaken."

His brown eyes pleaded with me. *"Please, Runa. Take this decision away from me. Just take my magic. I don't care as long as I'm with you."*

I felt like I'd been punched in the nose as tears streamed from my eyes.

"I'm trying to protect you, Konner. Do you think I want you to be with someone else? It crushes me to think of you with her, but this is the only way you can awaken. We just have to get through this." I pulled my copper key from around my neck and put it in his hand. *"Take this, and when the time comes, think of me. Pretend she's me. You can do it if it's me, right? I love you, and I need you to awaken."*

He clenched my key in his hand. *"I'll try."*

35

The following week, Kat made a feast to celebrate Rowan's and my promise to mate. The whole event was agony for Konner and uncomfortable for me and, therefore, Rowan. Kat, Ed, and Wilhelm didn't seem to notice.

"You must visit with the pups once they're born." Kat planned.

"I guess I know what you'll be doing at next year's Wolf Moon Festival," Wilhelm said under his breath to Rowan and me, grinning.

"Rowan, should we invite your parents over soon to meet Runa?" Kat asked.

"I think that can wait until it gets closer to Wilhelm's awakening," Rowan answered quickly.

Kat nodded. "Runa, be sure to come stay with us when the time comes for Wilhelm to awaken. It will be great to have you. Konner, you'll have to come home from university to visit at the same time."

A crippling sadness trickled through the bond,

and I knew Konner was trying unsuccessfully to keep it to himself.

It hurt to think I wouldn't see Konner after three weeks, but it was better that way. Even though I nodded at all of Kat's plans, I knew I wouldn't return to the farm once I'd left. If I did meet Rowan's parents before we were mated, we'd probably go to them. It would be far too painful to come back to the place where I had so many memories with Konner.

"It's really too bad Konner isn't mating right away," Kat lamented. "Oh well, there's still time, and I suppose there's always a chance Wilhelm will mate right after awakening. Maybe your children could be bondmates."

Wilhelm laughed. "Anything is possible."

The rest of the evening went similarly, and the three of us were relieved when it was late enough for bed. We stood and headed for the stairs.

"Wait." Kat stopped us. "It's traditional to kiss, isn't it?"

Ed smiled and nodded.

"Wooo, yeah! Kiss her, Rowan!" Wilhelm cheered.

I looked at Konner over Rowan's shoulder, and his eyes held back tears.

"Go on, what will it hurt?" Kat encouraged.

Rowan looked at me warily, and I sighed and nodded.

Konner, I love you. Please look away.

Rowan reached for me, and everyone held their breath in anticipation.

The kiss started as a gentle brush of our lips. But once my wolf felt her promised was near, she wanted to mark him as her own. I'm sure Rowan's wolf had the same idea. With the touch of Rowan's soft, warm lips on mine, my wolf demanded more. I pressed my lips insistently to his, and Rowan responded in kind. It wasn't for long, but our audience was convinced.

As I stepped away from Rowan, my insides quivered as Konner's pain crashed into me. *He didn't look away.*

When I'd crawled into Konner's bed that night, he turned his back to me. I reached for him but changed my mind. I felt guilty for what my wolf had done, but I was glad he hadn't told me to sleep alone.

As the days passed, I became even more conflicted. Konner was hurt, and it was my fault. I loved him and acutely felt his pain. My wolf, on the other hand, had gotten a taste of her promised, and she wanted more. Our nightly romps became more rambunctious, and our affectionate play was starting to leak into my time in human form. Konner suffered more every day, and Rowan acted less careful about muzzling his wolf. I don't know what else he could've done as his instincts became stronger and more insistent.

Everyone on the farm was busy with another harvest and planning for Konner's awakening.

Two weeks before Konner's awakening, Konner, Rowan, Wilhelm, and I were in the barn drying herbs. Konner and Wilhelm bound bundles of herbs in twine, and Rowan and I hung them to dry.

As Rowan and I returned to the workbench to grab more bundles, Rowan called to me.

I turned toward him to see what he wanted. He

reached up and tucked a purple flower into my hair. His tropical-water eyes sparkled down at me, and I couldn't help but smile back.

I picked up a handful of fallen buds and sprinkled them on his head, giggling at the sight.

"You're so pretty," Wilhelm said to Rowan.

"Don't be jealous."

"Pfft. I'm way prettier than you could ever dream of being," Wilhelm taunted.

I laughed at their banter and grabbed some bundles to hang. After carrying them to my step-stool, I climbed the steps with full arms.

Strong hands grasped my hips and steadied my wobbly ascent.

"Be careful," Rowan said apprehensively. "You shouldn't climb the stool with that many."

I looked down at him and smirked. "Are you worried about me, Rowan?" I teased, thinking his concerns were silly.

He gazed up at me seriously. "I don't know what I'd do if you got hurt."

My wolf wagged her tail with pleasure, but my smile faltered. I glanced over at Konner as he stood at the workbench. Though his back was to me, I could see his shoulders were tense, and he'd stopped bundling.

My heart sank, but I went back to work.

A lot of people visited in preparation for Konner's awakening. The fae priest came to go over the awakening ceremony as did the wolf mystic for the unbinding. Violet visited three times a week to ensure Konner would be comfortable when the time came.

I was about as happy with her visits as Konner was when I was with Rowan.

My alone-time with Konner was filled with strained silences. We both wanted to close the gap between us and reach for each other, but life's circumstances weighed heavily on us.

Every werewolf was on high alert as the Blood Moon neared. We heard howls every night to tell us someone had smelled a vampire. Luckily, no one was attacked.

A few days before Konner's awakening, I finally tried to reach out to him.

"I don't want to leave you like this, Konner. What can I do?"

His eyes were cool and distant; even my key around his neck was just a cold hunk of metal. He didn't bother to answer me.

While things between Rowan and I weren't as strained, the big question of whether we would go with Isla still hung over our heads. When Konner had refused to talk with me, I went outside to get some air. Rowan was loading fresh herbs into the handcart as Wilhelm cleaned up the workbenches in the barn.

I didn't intend to go to Rowan, but I somehow ended up there anyway.

"Hey, Runa." He smiled at me, then took in my expression. "What's wrong?"

Konner won't talk to me. "I don't know what I should do," I answered vaguely.

He opened his arms to me, but I remained where I stood, scuffing my boots on the ground. He looked disappointed but didn't push.

"He's awakening in a few days," he pointed out unnecessarily and fished for information.

I felt a pang in my heart.

"Have you decided if you'll go with Isla?"

"I don't know. Probably. I want to be with her and learn to be a better wolf. But leave Faerie? Live in the human realm? That's kind of a big step."

He nodded silently.

"Have you mentioned it to Wilhelm yet?"

He averted his eyes. "No, I only told him that Isla was rescued by wolves. You know Wilhelm, he wanted all the details. I had to dissuade him by saying they didn't tell us everything."

"Are you...do you know what you're going to do?"

He looked up at me, searching my eyes as if all the answers were there. "Do you want me to go with you, Runa?"

Yes. "I won't answer that. This has to be your decision. If I influence you one way or the other, you may end up resenting me."

He grabbed my hand, and I didn't resist. "I could never resent you. I love you."

Once again, I felt guilty as my wolf did a little dance. I looked away from his insistent eyes. "I can't help you decide. When we're mated, we can choose where we want to live together. But, for now, we each have to make the choice that's right for us as individuals."

"I want to be with you, Runa. You believe me, right? I know you'll have a hard time when you leave here without him. I want to help you heal. But Wilhelm...he needs me, too."

"I'm sorry you have to endure this pain. I wish

you never had to hurt. I want you to be happy. Whatever you choose, I'll follow your lead."

He wasn't happy, but he understood.

The day before Konner's awakening—and likewise the Blood Moon—dawned frigid. Even the sun was cold as it sparkled off the frozen morning dew. I was determined that Konner and I would come to terms and make amends. I asked him to follow me to the spring so we could talk.

"Konner, tomorrow is our last day together. Can we have happy memories of today?"

Konner finally broke. "Don't you want to spend it with Rowan?" he spat.

"Of course not. I want to spend it with you."

"You could've fooled me."

"What's that supposed to mean?"

"You've both been all over each other."

"That's not true."

"Every time you're together, you're close to one another, like you always have to be touching. I thought you said he'd control himself."

"I'm sorry. It's not entirely his fault though. I told you; it's instinct."

"That's not even a good lie."

"I'm not lying. You just don't understand what it means to be a wolf."

"If being a wolf means saying you love someone only to force that person to watch you mate another, you're right. I don't understand, but *you* sure are an expert."

My eyes started to well, and my voice broke when I said, "That's not fair, Konner. What was I supposed to do?"

"You could've picked anyone but him. If you

really loved me, you wouldn't have ever picked him."

His words drowned me, and I ran, leaving him raging.

My throat burned, and I couldn't swallow as I cried for what I'd done. I wasn't sure where I'd gone wrong. Was it when I fell in love with Konner? When I told him? When I made him promise to awaken? When I agreed to mate Rowan? By all standards I had ever been taught, agreeing to mate another wolf rather than running off with my bondmate was the only thing I'd done right.

But Konner doesn't feel that way. He feels betrayed, and my heart knows he's right.

At that point, there was little I could do. My time had run out, and I'd already vowed to mate Rowan. So I wallowed. I sobbed into my pillow until I was exhausted. Then I fell asleep.

36

I awoke from a dead sleep when terror slammed into the bond.

"Konner!" I screamed and raced into the bright afternoon sun.

I sprinted toward the spring, where I'd seen Konner last. He was nowhere in sight. A glint of copper caught my eye, and I ran toward it. My key lay on a broken chain on the ground amongst signs of a struggle. The chain was smeared in Konner's blood.

I took a deep breath through my nose, and there it was. Even in human form, I could smell the scent of damp earth and the sickening sweetness of a fresh vampire trail.

My heart stopped, then hammered in my chest.

"Konner?" I called through the bond.

No answer.

"Konner!"

Still nothing.

Not bothering to undress, I shifted and sounded the alarm with a heart-wrenching howl.

Then I followed the trail, calling Konner every few seconds. The scent was so fresh that it was overwhelming. It took a few minutes to determine the direction in which they'd gone. By that time, Rowan had answered my call with a howl, telling me that Wilhelm, Kat, and Ed were safely inside with him.

I ran through the woods, tracking the scent, calling Konner through the bond, and trying to keep my panic from distracting me. But, with every moment I couldn't find him, I was losing control.

When the trail had ended at a seemingly random tree, I circled it in an attempt to find the scent. I stared up into the branches and saw no sign that they were there.

I reached into the bond to get a general direction, but I couldn't feel anything except a sense of distance.

They must have taken him to the human realm. I don't have much time left.

As twilight fell, I returned to the farm. Everyone was grieving as if Konner was already dead.

Rowan followed me to my room to find out what had happened.

I put clothes in a bag and rolled it so it would fit in my wolf mouth once I shifted.

"It's all my fault, Rowan. I should never have left him alone."

"If you had been with him, they could've killed you, too."

"I'm going after him."

He grabbed my shoulders and forced me to look at him. "Runa, listen to me. Konner is dead."

"No, he isn't. I can still feel the bond."

"Then he soon will be. If you go after him, you won't survive."

"That's fine. If he dies, I don't want to live anyway."

Rowan's face twisted in agony. "Runa, please, don't do this. I can't watch my promised willingly run toward death."

"I understand." I stepped close to him. "Rowan, I release you from your promise and am thus released."

"Don't," he whispered as I leaned toward him. "Let's leave together. We can go to Isla and live with the pack. Runa, I love you." His ice-blue eyes were cracked like glass that would shatter with the lightest touch.

I kissed him gently on the mouth, and our wolf bond dissolved.

Tears flowed as his heart broke.

"I'm sorry, Rowan. Take care of yourself and Wilhelm, won't you?"

He dropped to his knees, hollow and beaten. I pushed away the grief I felt for him and shifted back to wolf form. I grabbed my bag in my mouth and ran as fast as I could toward town.

Having dissolved my promise to Rowan, I felt one again. Both my human and wolf hearts raced toward the one I loved.

The journey to town went a lot quicker as a wolf, though every second felt like an eternity.

I arrived at Zen's shop and shifted back to human form. Quickly dressing, I climbed the stairs that led to the second floor. I banged on the door until Zen answered.

"Runa, what—"

"No time to explain. I need you to get me through the veil to the human realm. Vampires snatched Konner."

Like Rowan, Zen looked sure Konner was already dead.

"He's alive, but we have to hurry."

Zen nodded once and stepped outside. As I followed him to the portal, he asked, "How will you find him once you're through?"

"I'm going to get help."

The portal wasn't far, but it took a while to get there because it was in the deepest part of a nearby forest. Lucky for me, Zen knew exactly where he was going. And there it was in an opening between two huge rocks. I wouldn't have even noticed it. But, as I stared with squinting eyes, the nearly full moon shimmered on the crevasse as if it were water.

I removed my clothes and stuffed them in the bag, leaving them nearby. Then I shifted and stepped up to the rippling door.

"Good luck, and come back safely," Zen encouraged.

I nodded and leapt through the veil.

The human realm didn't look much different, but the smell was completely off. I also heard unusual sounds in the distance, like a whistle and a metallic clanging.

I followed the slightly worn path in the forest floor, trotting toward my destination. After a few miles, I came upon a crossroads and turned left. It wasn't long before I smelled nearby werewolves. Eventually, the road ended at a large stone house.

I approached cautiously, not wanting to alarm anyone. I scratched at the wooden front door. I might've felt bad about scratching the wood had all the paint not been long peeled away. Finally, a burly werewolf in human form with too much facial hair answered the door. I couldn't tell through all the hair if he was surprised to find a wolf on his step or not.

I shifted to human form right in front of him. "I'm here to see Isla."

His dark eyes twinkled as he stepped aside to let me in. "You must be Runa."

I nodded and stepped inside. The house seemed to be a lodge of some sort with tall ceilings and exposed rafters. A few werewolves lounged around the open common area. Isla and Misha were cuddled up on a couch, reading.

"Runa!" Isla grinned. She untangled herself from her mate and approached me. She wrapped a couch blanket around my shoulders to cover my nakedness. None of the werewolves cared, but it was convention in the human realm. "Is Rowan with you?" she asked, concerned as she took in my expression.

"Isla, please listen. It's an emergency. Do you know where the vampires you've been tracking are in this realm?"

"We have a few ideas but nothing certain. Why?"

"They took Konner, and I'm here to get him back."

"That's way too dangerous, and our alpha

wouldn't sanction a raid without more information. Besides, we don't know exactly where they are. I'm sorry, Runa, but I think you should just let him go," she advised sympathetically.

"You don't understand. I love him."

All the werewolves' mouths hung open at my declaration. Some, like Isla, looked at me with pity. Others curled their lips in disgust.

"I see," Isla said quietly. "In that case, let's talk to Layton."

Misha and I followed Isla up a set of wooden stairs to the second floor. We walked down a long hallway with many doors on either side. She seemed to know exactly where to go as she knocked at a door somewhere in the middle.

"Come in," a rich voice called from the other side of the door.

We entered a study lined in well-stocked bookshelves. A deceptively elegant man with wavy chestnut hair and long, thin fingers smiled from behind a wide desk.

"Welcome. You must be Runa. I'm pleased you decided to join us."

"I'm sorry for the intrusion, Layton. Runa has something she'd like to ask," Isla explained.

Layton turned his full attention on me and smiled his encouragement.

"The vampires have stolen my bondmate. He's still alive. Could you tell me where to find them? I don't expect you to risk your pack's safety on such a dangerous mission. I can go in alone. I just need a location."

He answered in a reasonable tone. "If I let you go alone, I'd be sentencing you to death. Why would

I do that to a potential packmate? Furthermore, why would I risk any werewolf life to save one unimportant fae?"

"He isn't unimportant. He's the most important. I love him and will do whatever it takes to save him."

"You fell in love with your bondmate? How unusual though certainly not unheard of. As I'm sure Isla told you, we don't know their exact location. I'm afraid I can't be of much help."

"If you take me to the general area, I can get a location through the bond."

"Indeed? And you will go in without even knowing how many there are?"

"If Konner is conscious, I can ask him how many there are."

Layton was silent as he squinted in thought, tapping his finger against his lips.

"Layton?" Isla asked uncertainly.

A grin spread across his face. "This could be the break we've needed to destroy the nearby vampire infestation. Misha, assemble the pack. We're going hunting."

It didn't take long for the pack to assemble and be briefed. But, by the time everyone was ready, the sun had already begun lighting the sky in the east.

Ten wolves were going while a few stayed behind with the pups. We piled into a big van. The burly, hairy man, who I'd learned was named Clyde, operated the van while Layton sat beside him. I leaned against Isla in my borrowed clothes, and she cuddled me comfortingly.

I would've been amazed by the huge buildings and loud trains the humans had built if I hadn't been concentrating on locating Konner through the bond. As we drove through the bustling city, I could feel Konner getting closer.

Finally, Clyde stopped, and we all climbed out. The steamy alley we entered smelled horrible, like stale sewage and rusty metal.

"This is where we always lose the trail," Layton

explained. "Runa, can you tell which direction he's in?"

I closed my eyes and felt for Konner. *"Konner?"*

Still no response, but I got a vague idea of his location.

"He's underground. There must be someplace that leads below the street."

"The subway system?" Misha suggested.

Layton nodded thoughtfully. "We'd considered that possibility, but we had no way to navigate." He smiled at me. "Now, we do. All right everyone, look around for access to the subway lines."

We searched the alley for doors or service tunnel entrances.

"Over there." Isla pointed to a metal grate, through which hissing steam poured.

We went over, and Clyde lifted the grate easily.

"Runa, it's up to you to lead the way. Have you ever fought a vampire before?" Layton asked.

I dipped my head.

"Good, but I want you to leave that to us. Worry about finding Konner and getting out, okay?"

I nodded my understanding.

After we had all climbed down into the tunnel, Clyde shut the grate with a loud clang, and then everyone removed their clothes and shifted to wolf form.

I led the way, cautiously following where our bond pulled. The tunnels were dark and clouded with steam. They reeked of a metallic filth that made it impossible to smell the vampires. At every turn, I called to Konner. It took a long time before he answered.

"Runa?" His inner voice slurred as if he was disoriented. *"What are you doing here?"*

"Konner! I'm here to rescue you. Don't worry. I'm coming."

"No!" Panic sobered him. *"Get out. There are too many. They'll kill you. Leave me, and go home."*

"Not a chance. Besides, I've brought backup."

"Backup? What—"

"Konner, focus. How many are there?"

"Maybe eight?"

"We're coming to get you."

I shifted to human form and told the pack how many vampires Konner had seen. They smiled wolfy grins and nodded, and then I shifted back.

The tunnels had started as smooth industrial pipes. But, the farther we went, the older and cruder they became.

"Talk to me, Konner. What happened?"

"I'm sorry, Runa. It's all my fault. I was angry with you, so I didn't follow when you went inside. I took a walk to calm down. When I'd realized what a jerk I was being, I turned back to go home and apologize. I really am sorry. I know Rowan is your best option. If we get home, I won't make a fuss."

"No, Konner. I'm sorry. It was wrong to bond with Rowan in front of you, and this isn't your fault. Even if I was upset, I should never have left you alone."

"You couldn't help bonding with him. It was instinct."

"I could've tried harder to fight it." I was silent for a few moments, and then I added, *"I love you."*

"I love you, too."

The anxiety in my heart mixed with joy at his reply, and I doubled my determination to find him. *"What happened after you decided to come home?"*

"*Four vampires attacked me. I was taken completely by surprise. I felt a sharp pain in my neck as one of them bit me. I blacked out and awoke in a dirty stone room.*"

"*Why didn't they just kill you then?*" I wondered, not that I was upset at their choice.

"*I thought the same thing when I awoke tied to a chair. They only drink a sip from me at a time, something about saving me until I'll be the most delicious. I guess it really is a bad omen to be born on the Blood Moon. One of the vampires is more impatient, and another keeps telling him to wait until the moon rises.*"

"*How are they controlling themselves with the Blood Moon tonight and your magic as ripe as it can be?*"

"*I'd say barely.*"

As we got closer, we slowed our pace to a crawl, not wanting to alert the enemy to our approach.

My ears twitched at the echoes of the vampires talking.

"That's enough! It's my turn," one snarled

There was a scuffling sound, and Konner hissed in pain.

I rushed forward, but Layton cut me off, forcing me to approach slowly. I peeked around the corner into the hand-dug room as the pack prepared to attack.

Konner had miscounted. There were ten vampires, not eight. Nine stood anxiously around the dimly-lit room, eyes glowing in the lamplight as they waited for their turn to drink. The tenth sucked hungrily at Konner's raw neck. He surfaced for air and ran his tongue along Konner's throat. It glistened crimson with blood, and I stifled a growl and the urge to lunge.

"You are delicious, aren't you? Your magic must

be quite close to popping," he whispered to Konner like a lover.

I moved aside as Layton nudged me. I knew he wanted me to go in last, grab Konner, and get out. But, as the vampire smelled Konner's throat and whispered in his ear, I vowed to be the one to end him. The vampires were so concentrated on Konner that they never saw us coming. As soon as the growls and surprised shouts began, I launched myself at the vampire who I'd watched feed on Konner.

Since I was the last to enter, he was ready for me. He swatted me, and I flew against the wall. I shook the dazed feeling from my head and prepared to attack again. He crouched in a fighting stance and bared his teeth, which were still stained with Konner's blood.

This time, I was ready. All the training and preparation my parents and Rowan had given me paid off when I sank my teeth deep into his throat. I heard a gurgle, then a snap when I closed my jaw. The disgusting taste of dead blood squirted into my mouth while I shook my prey. I don't know how long it took to chew my way through the bone and muscle to remove the head, but I made sure that vampire was not coming back.

Revenge satisfied, I looked around the room to see if any wolves needed help. Some of them had already taken down their targets and others were holding their own. I shifted to human form and went to untie Konner's ropes.

"Konner?"

He didn't respond.

I checked his pulse as my own hammered in my fingertips. His heart was weak but still pumping.

The battle raged on around us as I pulled Konner onto my back. His feet dragged behind us while I carried him the way we'd come.

The sounds of growls and snapping teeth reverberated off the stone walls of the tunnel. When the echoes had faded with distance, I gently set Konner on the tunnel floor.

"Konner," I called aloud, tapping his cheek.

His eyes flew open and darted around wildly.

"Shhh, I'm here. You're all right."

He stared at the vampire's blood on my face. "And the vampires?"

"Busy getting shredded by Isla's pack."

His eyes filled with tears, and he tried to smile. "You came for me."

"Of course. Now, let's get you out of here. Can you walk with help?"

"I think so."

I hauled him to his feet and draped his arm around my shoulder.

"Runa, you're…you are…*naked*."

"If you're well enough to worry about that, I'd say you're in good shape."

We didn't get much farther before we heard the clicking of wolf claws on the stone floor. The pack overtook us not long after. They were bloody, beaten, and limping, but they were all there. I sighed in relief.

"You all made it." I smiled.

Layton shifted to human form. "And it's thanks to both of you that we were able to find and surprise them."

"Anything I can do to help," Konner murmured.

Layton laughed and helped support Konner's other side. "Indeed."

The most difficult part of our trek was getting Konner through the grate to the surface. But with Clyde's help, it wasn't too bad.

Konner was able to stay conscious long enough to marvel at the human city that towered above us and to climb into the van.

I stroked his matted hair as his head rested on my shoulder on the ride back to the pack lodge.

When we'd arrived, those who'd stayed behind quickly attended to the injured. I had a bump on my head but was, otherwise, all right. One careful old woman cleaned and bandaged Konner's neck wounds. Then Clyde carried Konner to a guest room. I followed, unwilling to leave his side.

*J*didn't realize I'd fallen asleep until I felt a warm hand stroke my cheek. I startled awake, and Konner smiled at me from where he lay on the bed.

"How are you?" I asked, standing from my bedside chair and stretching.

"I'm happy to be back with you."

His sentiment reminded me that it was the day of his awakening. I rushed to the window and threw open the curtains. The Blood Moon shone brightly through the glass.

"Konner, I'm sorry," I said, feeling like I'd failed him. "We won't be able to get back to Faerie before your awakening. At sunrise, your magic will be lost, and it'll be my fault."

"No," he hushed me. "We share the blame. I have to apologize as well. Since I won't awaken, you won't be able to join wolf society. Your future with Rowan is—"

"I have no future with Rowan." I cut him off.

"That's what I'm saying. I'm sorry I ruined it."

I sat beside him on the bed. "No, I'm no longer Rowan's promised. I dissolved our bond before I left Faerie."

"Why?"

"Many reasons, but mostly because I never would've been able to reconcile my wolf instincts and my human emotions if I'd mated him."

He sat up slowly, staring at me with clear eyes. "Runa, will you be my mate?"

"What? Konner, it's forbidden."

"I don't care. You can't go back to wolf society anyway, and I don't want to live without you. We could stay in the human realm. Without my magic, maybe I won't be appetizing to vampires."

I stared at him, stunned and torn.

"Runa, please. I love you, and I want to be your mate." His brown eyes pleaded with me, offering everything I ever wanted but didn't let myself have.

I leaned forward and kissed him earnestly. "I love you," I whispered. "You'll never wish for a better mate than me."

He grinned like a fool and kissed me with gusto. Our joy soon turned to passion, having caged our desire for too long. Our kisses became insistent, but I broke contact and held him at arm's length.

"Wait. You're injured."

"I'm not *that* injured."

I didn't resist when he crushed me to him just to show he had enough strength.

I trailed my lips possessively down his throat, gently placing kisses over the bandage.

"I've waited so long," he gasped as I splayed my hands over his stomach and chest.

I climbed on top of him, straddling his hips, and pulled off my shirt.

There was no embarrassed blush on his cheeks when he reached for my breasts. There was only the flush of need.

I encouraged his exploration as he touched my skin in fascination. My desire had been shackled long enough. When he started to grind his hard cock against my core, I knew he was ready.

I slowly removed the rest of our clothes, and we worshiped the sight of each other.

When I'd climbed on top of him again, he rolled me onto my back. I smiled up at him, and he bent down to kiss my face and neck.

I stared deep into his eyes as I reached down and guided his blunt tip to where it needed to be.

"I love you," I breathed.

His eyes were glazed with lust when he whispered, "I love you."

Then he thrust his cock deep into me, and we both moaned our appreciation.

He cradled me close, and I clutched his back as he drove us to our mutual completion. When he finally pumped inside me, an unusual green aura surrounded us. It glowed brightly, then disappeared.

We stared at each other in shock.

"Um, that doesn't normally happen. Was that…"

"My awakening," he finished in a hushed tone. He muttered a few words in ancient Elvish, and pink fae lights appeared and floated around the room.

I beamed at him. "I read that you have to trust your guide when you become one. It said timing mattered, but it didn't specify that your guide had to be fae." I laughed. "With fae and werewolf matings being forbidden, they probably didn't want anyone to know." I met his eyes. "Happy birthday, Konner," I whispered.

Joy hummed through the bond.

"Konner, the bond is still there."

"So?"

"So do you really want your mate to know what you're thinking and feeling all the time?"

"I don't mind."

"But...if we aren't unbound, we can never have children."

"Do you want children?"

"I don't know. Is it even possible? If I do have children, I want them to be yours."

He smiled at me giddily. *"Well, I guess we'll just have to be unbound when we're mated."*

"I don't mind if it's just us for a while though. I have a lot I want to do first,"

He grinned. *"Do you? And when would you like to start this journey?"*

I let my desire flow through the bond. *"Right now."*

EPILOGUE

Dearest Runa,

How are you? I'm doing well with the northern pack. My days are long, but I'm finally starting to realize what we were missing in Faerie.

As for my promise to fall in love again, it's not going so well. But I don't mind right now. I have plenty of time and a lot more to learn about being a better wolf.

My job at the café is coming along. I even have regular customers who remember me and call me by name. Most of them are very nice and always greet me with a smile. But there is one college girl who comes every day after class. She really irritates me. It's like she always has something snide to say to me, and she never calls me by my name. Why does she keep coming if she hates me so much? Sometimes, humans are more difficult to understand than fae.

Runa, I haven't forgotten you, but I'm in a bad

*place when I think of you. It hurts too much to see
you, but the longing hurts even more.*

*I'm sure you're reading this with that same look
of pity. Please don't. I don't write this to hurt you but
to tell you where I am. You asked for updates.*

*I know I'm being selfish, but expressing my feel-
ings makes them more bearable even if I know you
don't feel the same.*

*I'm trying. I'm trying to see you as only a friend
so we can be together without it being painful. I so
want to be your friend.*

*Have faith in me. As always, you will never need a
better friend than me. Call for me, and I'll come whenever for whatever.*

*I better go to sleep now. I have work early tomor-
row. Sweet dreams, Runa.*

Still yours,
Rowan

PS Tell Konner I'll rip his throat out if he hurts you.

I folded the letter and put it in my jacket pocket. My heart hurt as it always did when I'd heard from Rowan. Still, I smiled at his lack of awareness and promised to write back.

"Konner, are you ready?" I called from outside our small cottage in the woods.

He appeared from inside and shut the door behind him. "I'm sorry. I wanted to grab my gift for Zehra. I forgot it last time, and I didn't want to disappoint her again."

I shook my head at him. "You spoil her."

"So what? That's why I'm her favorite."

I handed him a backpack full of human goods, and we headed down the trail toward the portal to Faerie, holding hands.

The autumn air was crisp but refreshing, and fallen leaves crunched under our feet. I took a deep breath, enjoying the earthy smell. Gazing at Konner, I saw the copper glint of my key peek out from under his auburn scarf.

"I got a letter from Rowan."

"Is he still in love with you?"

I sighed sadly and nodded.

"Is he still going to rip my throat out?"

"Of course."

He laughed. "Well, don't be too hard on him. You're difficult to forget."

"I don't want him to forget me. I just want him to move on and find love with someone else. Then maybe we can be friends."

"Maybe you're asking for too much."

"I don't think so. Besides…" I grinned. "It seems a human has taken an interest in him."

"Oh? And what does Rowan think?"

"He's oblivious. He thinks she hates him for no reason, but she's getting under his skin. That could be a start."

"Why does he think she hates him?"

"Because she teases him. If she really hated him, she wouldn't go to his café every day."

"Wow, every day? He *is* oblivious."

We walked in companionable silence, breathing the fresh air and listening to the autumn birds sing.

Zen waited for us by the portal. He smiled and waved a greeting.

We handed him our packs, and he paid us.

"Did you find everything?" he asked.

I nodded. "All except the flashlight."

"You couldn't find a flashlight?"

"Oh, I did, but then Konner shorted it out. I'll get another one for next time."

Konner shrugged. "It's not my fault magic messes with electronics. Runa gets to play with all the cool stuff."

Zen laughed good-naturedly. "It really is helpful having werewolves to collect and display all the neat human gadgets."

"I do what I can."

"How's your book about living in the human realm coming, Konner?"

"It needs some work, but I'm happy with it so far."

"That's good. Let me know when you're ready to submit it to the publisher."

"Thanks. I will."

Zen pulled a letter from his jacket and handed it to Konner. "From your mother," he explained. "I guess Wilhelm and Arete will be mated soon, and she wants you to come home for the ceremony."

"I bet," Konner said dryly.

"Oh, come on. Don't be like that," I scolded.

"Did you forget last time? She held us hostage for three days."

"Now, you're just being dramatic."

Zen laughed at our shenanigans and gave me the list of goods to get for next month. "See you later," he called before stepping through the veil.

We turned and started toward the pack lodge, where we were dining that night.

As we approached, a young werewolf with long, cream-colored hair sprinted from the house and launched herself into Konner's arms.

"Uncle Konner!"

"Zehra!" he shouted, matching her enthusiasm and hugging her tightly.

"For goodness sakes, you saw each other last week." I laughed at them.

"I think Aunt Runa is jealous. Maybe you should give her a kiss."

Zehra smiled at me with dimpled cheeks as she kissed me. "I missed you too, Aunt Runa."

"Aw, and I missed you, Zehra."

She turned to Konner excitedly. "Did you bring it?"

"Who do you think I am?" he scoffed.

Then he pulled a small, corked vial on a cord out of his pocket. He'd enchanted green glitter to swirl around the vial. He put the cord around her neck, and she watched in rapture as the glitter danced.

Then she dashed toward the house yelling, "Mama, Mama, Uncle Konner gave me some of his fairy dust!"

Isla appeared at the sound of her daughter's excited screams. She looked at the vial, then at Konner. "You spoil her, Konner." She smiled her thanks.

He feigned shock as we headed into the lodge. "Why does everyone say that?"

I laughed. "Because it's true. I don't even want to know how spoiled our children will be."

"It's called payback," Isla joked.

"I guess we'll soon find out." Konner beamed at me and rubbed my barely pregnant belly.

"I guess we will." I kissed him affectionately and went to greet the rest of the pack.

Read on for an excerpt from
D. Lieber's Intended Fates

Intended Strangers

Available now in
ebook, paperback, and hardcover

Silvery moonlight streamed in through the windowless frames of the derelict factory. I caught a glimpse of the waning crescent in a cracked antique mirror beside me, but its light wasn't strong enough to bounce to the one facing it.

The eyes of my reflection glowed with eyeshine as the moonlight hit them just right. My black fur was raised along my spine, but I managed to silence the growl that tried to climb up my throat.

My nose twitched at the stench that hung in the air—damp and rich, like dark earth with the sickly sweet undertone of fresh decay. The disgusting scent of vampire likely wouldn't leave my nose for days to come.

The many mirrors, arranged like a twisted funhouse, confused my sight while I scanned the space. The effect made me dizzy as I searched for any motion that wasn't us.

My packmates were on either side of me, a few steps ahead. Grant's tail was stiff as he stalked slowly forward; Aryn stepped so quietly that her nails didn't make a sound on the concrete floor.

Our soft, mingled breaths were the only sound my strained ears picked up. If it wasn't for the strength of that awful smell, I might have thought Grant had gotten the location wrong.

Perhaps they're out hunting for the night. But I threw that thought away a moment after it came to my mind. Grant wouldn't have called me here if he suspected the hunt would be fruitless.

A gentle whiff of air brushed the tips of my ears. I looked up just in time to see my enemy descend from above. Its pale, bloodless skin appeared out of the darkness as it jumped down from the rusted rafters.

I sprang out of the way just in time, and Grant and Aryn whirled around to face the threat that had finally showed itself. It almost seemed to smile, its sharp teeth clicking as it gnashed them.

I let loose the growl I'd been holding in, my lips vibrating with the force of it. My packmates echoed my sentiment. But just as I was bunching my muscles to spring, two more vampires came up behind me. I twisted around, leaving the one in front of me to Grant and Aryn, but I wasn't quick enough. Something flashed in one of the new arrival's hands, and a searing pain erupted from my side as it slashed at me.

I didn't let it get away so easily. I grabbed its forearm, still outstretched from its attack, and sank my teeth in. Dead blood leaked into my mouth, and the thing hissed its pain. I yanked it down to the floor, my jaws closing on its jugular in less than a minute.

Once its strangled cries had ceased, I turned my attention back to my packmates. They had fared just as well, their quarries deader than they had been before we'd gotten there.

Grant shifted to human form and stood naked before us. "That should be all of them."

Aryn shifted as well. "It's a good thing they were so newly turned, or it might have been a real challenge."

Now that the fight was over, the fiery pain of my injury pulsed through me with every heartbeat. I shifted with difficulty; never had the action been painful before. "Speak for yourself," I wheezed.

Thanks to the many mirrors, I got a panoramic view of the damage. A nasty gash ran from just below my left pec over my ribs. The cut wasn't deep, but it was bleeding and the edges were turning blue. "That can't be good." My voice sounded far away, as if it belonged to someone else.

My reflection looked the worse for wear. His black hair stuck up at odd angles, and his ice-blue eyes seemed unfocused. His broad shoulders were slick with sweat, and his solid legs trembled beneath him. His strong jaw and straight nose did nothing to hide what he was feeling as his face twisted in pain.

My head spun and the ground went out from under me before becoming a nice, cool compress against my backside.

I didn't know quite what was going on, but I got a sense of flurried activity. A few minutes later, I felt a sharp prick in my arm, and reality rushed back into focus.

"What the hell was that?" I groaned, cold sweat and the concrete floor making me shiver.

"The mirrors." Grant recapped the needle of a syringe. "I do *not* miss the days of silver-backed mirrors. That must've been what it cut you with."

"But don't worry." Aryn smiled as she sat cross-legged beside me. "We always pack an antidote in the van just in case. You'll be fine in a few minutes. The wound itself might take a day longer to heal, but you won't even have a scar."

They were right. In a few minutes, I felt normal again, despite the gash, which Aryn had cleaned and covered while I'd been down.

"Well, we better get this done before sunrise." Grant rose to a stand. "It'll be that much harder to take care of the bodies once the humans are up and about."

I stood, glad my legs weren't wobbly anymore.

Aryn frowned. "I think we can handle them ourselves. Don't you, Grant? Rowan doesn't need to stay any longer."

I opened my mouth to protest, but Grant cut me off.

"She's right. You have work on Monday, right? We appreciate your coming out to help us. A one-to-one ratio is so much easier."

"And safer," Aryn added.

"And safer," Grant agreed. "But take today and tomorrow to heal. We can clean up here."

I didn't like the idea of leaving my packmates to take care of the rest, but they were right. They were the experienced hunters in this realm. I was just an auxiliary when they needed an extra set of teeth, and that was hardly ever since they often teamed up with wolves from other packs. I wasn't nearly on the same level as they were, not yet anyway. But that's to be expected when they got to grow up in a pack their whole lives and I didn't.

Despite this little mishap, I was good at hunting, though protecting had been the focus of most of my training, so I was much better at that. Even so, I had a lot to learn. And if my wound could heal before I went back to work on Monday, all the better—one less thing to have to lie to my boss about.

"All right." I wouldn't argue.

We headed back to the van we'd parked earlier in the night and dressed in the clothes we'd left in it. Grant gave me directions to where I could pick up a taxi to the airport. I said goodbye, wished them good luck, and headed back home to the ski resort.

AFTERWORD

Thank you for reading! I do so hope you enjoyed it. If you have a moment, I would very much appreciate a review on the store where you bought it. Tell other readers what you thought, and help them make a decision on this book.

If you'd like to stay updated on news about my books and events, you can subscribe to my newsletter on my website: www.dlieber.com

On my site, you will also find my blog, where I post all my fun little tidbits.

Thanks again! I hope you will travel through my worlds with me again in the future.

D. Lieber

ABOUT THE AUTHOR

D. Lieber has a wanderlust that would make a butterfly envious. When she isn't planning her next physical adventure, she's recklessly jumping from one fictional world to another. Her love of reading led her to earn a Bachelor's in English from Wright State University.

Beyond her skeptic and slightly pessimistic mind, Lieber wants to believe. She has been many places—from Canada to England, France to Italy, Germany to Russia—believing that a better world comes from putting a face on "other." She is a romantic idealist at heart, always fighting to keep her feet on the ground and her head in the clouds.

Lieber lives in Wisconsin with her husband (John) and cats (Yin and Nox).

Links:
Website: www.dlieber.com
Goodreads: www.goodreads.com/dlieberwriting
BookBub: https://www.bookbub.com/profile/d-lieber